She took his hand and placed it on her belly.

Once again, Stacy was struck with the oddity of their situation. She'd never imagined that her first baby, her first marriage, would start off this way. With a stranger that she was getting to know more every day. This was a good thing. She had to know the father of her child. Assure herself she was doing the right thing.

Adam's warm hand settled on her stomach. This made the second time he'd touched her so close to the part of her anatomy that caused this situation in the first place. It disturbed her that the small touch sent heat spiraling through her.

"What does it feel like when she moves?"

"I don't think you'll feel it. It's small, like a flutter. Kind of like butterfly wings."

When Adam met her gaze, hand on her stomach, his eyes shimmered with tenderness. The heat surged deeper, stronger, and tugged at the part of her she'd sworn wouldn't get involved.

She'd told herself that Adam's heart wasn't available.

But maybe it was hers.

Dear Reader,

Welcome to a Charming, Texas, Christmas. I know you're not surprised that in this quirky town, the locals are over-the-top about the holiday. Twinkling lights are in such high demand that they quickly sell out. The chamber of commerce hosts the annual tree-lighting ceremony, and sailboats launch for the sixtieth annual Christmas float boat snowflake parade.

You might remember Adam Cruz from *The Charming Checklist*, a former member of the SEAL special force team. Like his friends, he's no longer active duty. Unlike his friends, Adam hasn't quite found his footing in the intervening years. A widower struggling with PTSD, he's bounced from one job to another, finally winding up in Charming with his buddies. But before he leaves Montana, Adam leaves something important behind.

Our heroine, Stacy Hartsell, has that very tiny something with her. She arrives in Charming to tell Adam their one-night stand resulted in an accidental pregnancy, but she doesn't expect anything from him. She's on her way to Chicago to move in with her mother and create the support system every single mother needs. Imagine her surprise when Adam wants to be involved, enough to suggest a marriage of convenience!

How do two people who barely know each other create a family? Let's just say it doesn't hurt to have friends and the help of a few adorable senior citizens who know just how precious true love can be.

I hope you enjoy Adam and Stacy's whirlwind romance!

You can contact me at heatherly@heatherlybell.com.

Happy reading,

Heatherly Bell

A Charming Christmas Arrangement

HEATHERLY BELL

HARLEQUIN
SPECIAL
EDITION

HARLEQUIN®
SPECIAL
EDITION™

Recycling programs for this product may not exist in your area.

ISBN-13: 978-1-335-72417-5

A Charming Christmas Arrangement

For questions and comments about the quality of this book, please contact us at CustomerService@Harlequin.com.

Harlequin Enterprises ULC
22 Adelaide St. West, 41st Floor
Toronto, Ontario M5H 4E3, Canada
www.Harlequin.com

Printed in U.S.A.

Heatherly Bell tackled her first book in 2004, and now the characters that occupy her mind refuse to leave until she writes them a book. She loves all music but confines singing to the shower these days. Heatherly lives in Northern California with her family, including two beagles—one who can say hello and the other a princess who can feel a pea through several pillows.

Books by Heatherly Bell

Harlequin Special Edition

Charming, Texas

Winning Mr. Charming
The Charming Checklist

Wildfire Ridge

More than One Night
Reluctant Hometown Hero
The Right Moment

Harlequin Superromance

Heroes of Fortune Valley

Breaking Emily's Rules
Airman to the Rescue
This Baby Business

Visit the Author Profile page
at Harlequin.com for more titles.

For Amy Lamont, my first author friend,
who loves Christmas and would love it year-round.

Amy, I'll see what I can do about that.

Chapter One

In a perfect world, it would not be this difficult to find the father of her baby.

Blame it on the fact that Stacy Hartsell barely knew the man. All on her. But she'd checked with his employer, and Adam Cruz no longer worked on a goat farm in Marion. She could count the things she knew about the man on one hand. Things like the fact that he had large, callused, but surprisingly gentle hands. That he'd been kind and loving for one incredible night. And his eyes. They were a deep and dark brown—the saddest eyes she'd ever seen. She'd never forget those eyes.

"I tried." Stacy rested a hand on her expanding belly. December had entered Montana like a force of nature, and the wind had turned sharp and bitterly cold overnight. Tomorrow, she'd start the first leg of her drive home to Chicago. Her mother, Regina, a nurse, would help with the baby once "she" was born. Stacy held on to that hope for a girl, even though at her sixteen-week ultrasound recently, the technician claimed it was too soon to tell.

Still, so much had gone wrong in her life for the last few years. She'd made too many mistakes. The very least fate could do was give her a sweet baby girl out of this hot mess.

"We're in this together, sweetheart, you and me. It's just us."

Stacy sealed up another box of books and just as the tape made its loud scrape against the cardboard, she heard a knock on her front door. She wasn't expecting anyone and had already said goodbye to her only friend in Montana.

Stacy opened the door, and sure enough, there stood Grace, holding two coffees from the shop where they'd originally met.

"Decaf for you." Grace waltzed in, bringing some of the biting cold with her.

"Thanks." Stacy accepted the cup. "But I thought we weren't going to do this."

"Get all sad and maudlin? We're not."

"I write thrillers. I'd rather kill you than cry with you."

They'd met while writing in the same coffee shop in downtown Marion. It had taken three weeks to figure it out, but when Stacy noticed Grace staring off into space, she'd put it all together. Daydreamer. Fellow writer. After three years alone in Montana, the last six months researching and writing her second book, she'd found her people.

"I bring good tidings to you."

Grace was that most dangerous of all writers: a romance writer. Full of hope, brimming with romance and a strange real-life belief in happily ever after. God bless her. Stacy would sure miss her.

"I'm leaving tomorrow." Stacy plopped down on the couch. The cottage had come fully furnished, making it easy enough to leave everything behind. "And I did try to find him. He's in the wind."

"That may be true." Grace joined her on the couch. "But you've forgotten one tiny detail about me."

"What's that? That you don't believe in writer's block?" Stacy snorted.

"Oh, you're so darned cute. No. You should remember how I *love* my research."

"I do remember." Stacy took a sip of her decaf mocha latte. "Like that time you missed your deadline, too busy falling down the rabbit hole of Scottish castles."

"But I've solved your problem." She pulled a piece of paper out of her purse, held it up and waved it like a flag. "Ta-da!"

"What's that? Today's word count?"

Grace elbowed Stacy. "You won't believe this!"

Hope spiked through Stacy. "Oh, gosh, did I win?"

The coffee shop held a drawing only their regulars knew about. A week's worth of free coffee. It would be just her luck to win now.

"I found Adam." Grace tucked the slip of paper in Stacy's hand. "In Texas."

Until that moment, Stacy thought she was done. She'd tried to find Adam. It wasn't her fault he'd left town. She unfolded the paper and glanced down at the address of the post office in Charming, Texas. Last she'd heard, that was part of the Gulf Coast. The very bottom of Texas.

"He's having all his mail forwarded there," Grace said.

Stacy supposed she *could* drive to the post office in Charming and ask if they knew where she might find her baby's daddy. Surely, stranger things had happened. Though she couldn't think of any at the moment, aside from the plot twists she wrote into her thrillers.

"Stacy? Honey? Say something."

Adam hadn't seemed like the kind of man who would welcome news of impending fatherhood. Instead, he'd been…a little damaged. Lost. He'd drawn her in that special night with his hard-muscled, rough cowboy exterior, soothing voice and warm eyes.

The whole crazy night had been *her* idea.

And then, the next morning, she'd had the equivalent of her teeth knocked in by a roundhouse punch. She was still too embarrassed to mention it to Grace.

"I mean, um…" Stacy began.

"He deserves to know. You said you would tell him."

"I said I'd *try*, and I did! Grace, this isn't going to go the way you hope it will."

"You don't know that."

"Do you know how far *Texas* is out of my way?"

"You really shouldn't drive, anyway. I've been worried about that. Let us go in together and buy you an airplane ticket."

"And what about my car? I can't leave it here." There were twenty-four payments left on the economy sedan.

"Well, Charming is about thirty-one hours from Marion. If you take stops along the way, Texas is just a little farther south than you were intending to drive, anyway."

"A little?" She snorted. "Do you have any idea how *big* Texas is?"

"Some idea," Grace said. "But I hope you're about to find out."

Stacy couldn't blame Grace, who didn't have all the facts. Her friend didn't have any idea that she wanted to send Stacy to tell a man, still hung up on another woman, that he'd knocked up his one-night stand. That now he'd be a father.

Yeah.

That should go well.

"Oh, my gosh, I love Christmas!" Ava Long seemed poised to levitate with excitement. "Don't you?"

Out of the corner of his eye, Adam caught his best friend, Max Del Toro, giving his fiancée the cut-it-out sign. Sure, because Adam was apparently still so "precious" that everyone tiptoed around him. He hated *that* more than he hated Christmas. And he didn't hate the holiday as much as he preferred to ignore it.

"I do love Christmas." Adam slid Ava a smile, and sent Max a glare. "Why not."

Max gave him a patient look. "Of course, you do."

Just before opening, Max and Ava were trimming the tree they'd put in a corner of the Salty Dog Bar and Grill. Boxes of ornaments, wreaths and strings of lights were scattered on the floor. By his estimate, and judging by his own height, this tree was a good twelve feet tall.

"Where in Texas did you find this tree?" It was a Douglas fir, reminding Adam a bit of the ones he'd seen in the Montana mountains not long ago.

"Oh, I ordered it a while back."

"It isn't real?" He leaned in and, sure enough, no pine smell. Seemed criminal.

"Fresh trees are a fire hazard." Max finished stringing lights over the top of the tree.

"This is safer." Ava handed Max another strand. "I was disappointed, too, but Max has a point."

This was probably better for Adam. At least the smell of pine wouldn't pull more memories out of him. The therapist he'd seen after Mandy's sudden death said that flashbacks came from all five senses.

But Adam couldn't just stand there, so he joined in, helping string the lights around the fake tree. Next came ornaments, some ceramic, some plastic. When he picked up a ceramic one that said, "First Christmas," a sharp memory hit him of the first and only time he'd put up a tree with his new wife. They'd only had one holiday together.

Still, this would be the third Christmas without Mandy. It irritated him he still kept track this way. One Christmas without Mandy, two Christmases without Mandy, three… It had been almost four years since she'd been gone. He should have moved on, and she would have wanted him to. Yet every time he even glanced at another woman, he felt as if he was cheating.

And he'd already "cheated" on her once, though not technically. The enticing memory, from four months ago, came wrapped in guilt. Still, the memory helped get him through some of his worst days. Try as he might, he'd never regret that one night, despite all the corresponding and inexplicable guilt. Stacy Hartsell had dropped into his life to temporarily remind Adam he was still alive. That he could still feel…something.

But it sure didn't feel like Christmas this year. The weather didn't help. In Montana, it would be snowing. He'd been told by the Charming locals that the weather was cooler than normal for this time of year. A mere seventy-four. The sun gleamed on them every day with no intention of dulling. No rain yet, though it kept being promised. But he'd been all over the world with the Navy SEALs, and for him the weather didn't mean a thing. Only the calendar mattered, ticking away the days.

And the calendar said that Adam was another year older and still hadn't moved on.

Once it was time to clock in and prep in the kitchen for the day, Adam left Max and Ava to the tree. He had work to do in his kitchen. When his best friends and former SEAL team members had purchased a bar and grill in Charming, Adam's curiosity had been piqued. Not enough to come up and visit. He'd been fine on the goat farm, after all, keeping to himself. The hard physical work tired him out every day. Left little time to think and dwell.

Then, Max had called, said he'd fired his head cook and was in a jam. Would he help a brother out? That's how Adam wound up as the head fry cook of a bar and grill in the bucolic town of Charming on the Gulf Coast. As he chopped sweet potatoes and vegetables, and started a soup base, he kept his mind on work. The staff trickled in, and soon talking and laughing rang through the air. Coffee percolated, the rich smell wafting to the kitchen and mixing with the smells of bacon, fried potatoes and eggs.

The mood was light, probably due to Christmas looming. Two of his coworkers, Sam and Brian, arrived, calling out greetings and getting to work immediately. They'd found a solid groove within the first few days. These dudes were hard workers who ran circles around Adam when it came to speed. But he cooked better than any of them. He'd developed a

sixth sense when a dish needed a little extra season-
ing or a little more butter—just the right amount, no
more and no less. Mandy had taught him how to cook
and before long he was better than her.

And there went the ache again. A tightness that
made him stop flipping a pancake and rub his chest.
The therapist said it was more than grief—it was
guilt that made it tough for Adam to move on. His nature made him think he could save everyone, fix everything. Not true. He couldn't save Mandy, though
he'd tried.

"Isn't it time for your break, boss?" Sam asked.

Right again. Sometimes Adam got so caught up
he lost track of time. "Yeah. I'll just make myself a
lunch and grab an empty booth."

"You ought to take a walk down the wharf and
get some fresh air."

Great. Even his young coworkers were worried
about him. He was going to have to start making
more of an effort at socializing.

"Maybe I will."

"I'll take care of your lunch. Go grab a seat. I'll
have Debbie bring it to you."

Before they kicked him out, Adam pulled off his
apron and headed out. The lunch crowd began to
arrive. Couples laughing and chatting, some with
shopping bags from the stores along the wharf. Max
and Ava, done with the tree, now sat at a table making googly eyes at each other. Adam decided then
that he'd go ahead and ask out Twyla, since she'd

expressed interest in him on day one. His heart wasn't in it, but something Ava had said one evening stuck with him: fake it 'til you make it. Someday it wouldn't be this hard.

Before the two lovebirds saw Adam and asked him to sit with them, he scanned the room for a free table…and that's when he saw *her*. Sitting alone, watching him, biting her lower lip, eyes wide.

Sweet memory, front and center. Was he *seeing* things? It sure looked like Stacy. Long, dark hair and blue eyes. A smile that never failed to tug one out of him. The only woman he'd biblically *known* since Mandy. But that couldn't be, because she lived in Marion, and…

"Adam." She waved him over.

Well, this settled it. *Stacy* was here. Now. He couldn't deny the excitement that thrummed through him.

He headed to her booth. "Hey. What are you doing here?"

The smile slipped off her face as she stood. "I—I had to see you."

She looked exactly as he'd remembered her in all his fantasies—still gorgeous, though she'd gained a little weight. Interestingly, though, only in her stomach…

Suddenly every sound in the room stopped and everything faded to black. He could no longer smell French fries and burgers cooking. Every sensory awareness tuned into his vision, which focused on

Stacy's abdomen like a laser beam. This…couldn't be happening. He swallowed, a sudden thickness in his throat.

Her cheeks flushed pink as he scanned her body and fixated on her swollen belly. When she protectively lowered her hand, every question he'd had was answered. Except for one.

"Is it…mine?" The sound of his own voice was a small croak.

She nodded, biting her lower lip. The knowledge slammed into him.

Merry Christmas!

This was one heck of an early present.

Chapter Two

Stacy sat, having achieved her mission without the use of words. Awkward. One look at her and Adam had put it all together. She didn't want to shock him, but *showing* him seemed far better than hemming and hawing and catching up before she finally revealed the truth. After only one night together, they were basically strangers. Now, they would be parents.

Adam no longer had his beard and long, unruly locks. He wore his hair short, almost a military-style crew cut. No beard except for hints of dark bristle. It was a wonder she recognized him, but those eyes were unforgettable.

He took a seat across the booth and stared at her,

as if he was wondering if he could be dreaming all this. "How've you been?"

"Um, well, a little busy." She studied the plaid tablecloth. "Since… I found out."

"Right."

For another few minutes they didn't speak. Stacy continued to study the pattern of the tablecloth. Excruciating.

"Here you go." A waitress placed a plate in front of Adam. She turned to Stacy. "Change your mind? Would you like something to eat after all?"

"No, thank you."

All Stacy wanted to do was find a motel and sleep for a day. This road trip hadn't been easy. After sleeping, tomorrow she'd start the drive to Chicago. She shouldn't have let Grace talk her into this detour. Maybe a letter to him would have been enough. But there was a niggling doubt in the back of her mind. Maybe Adam wouldn't believe her. Or, she thought as she swallowed painfully, *remember* her. Because the night had been memorable to her didn't mean it had been the same for him.

Adam pushed his plate toward her. "Here. Please, eat."

"No. That's *your* lunch."

"I'm not hungry." He drummed his fingers on the table. "And you need it more than I do."

"Um, okay." She bit into a warm French fry, because this morning she'd had a stale donut for breakfast and horrible decaf coffee.

Adam raked a hand through his hair, and she could see his knee jiggling with nervous energy. Finally, she took pity on him, and went into her prepared speech.

"I wanted you to know, because you have a right. But I don't need you to be involved or feel responsible for us. I have a plan. It's not fair to spring this on you, and obviously neither one of us planned for this. I've had time to get used to the idea and I'm going through with it. But I don't expect anything from you."

He narrowed his eyes. "That's okay. I expect it from myself."

So he was going to be one of *those* guys. Honorable to a fault. Or was the right word *controlling*? He couldn't just start calling the shots now. No way. She would go to Chicago, where her mother would help. After all, Stacy had a book to finish, and a contract to honor. And she'd like to finish the book before midnight feedings took over her life. Eventually, she'd figure out a way to have her writing career and be a single mom. Her mother had been a single mom and so could Stacy.

"That's nice of you. But I'm on my way to Chicago, where I'll stay until the baby is born, and probably after, too. I'm a writer so I can work from anywhere."

"I remember."

It was all he knew about her. "Fiction, mostly."

"Thrillers." He nodded. "I will help with the baby, of course. Anything you need."

"I know you didn't plan on any of this but neither did I. Hey, merry Christmas, kind of early."

He ignored her lame joke. "I'll take care of you, too."

She snorted, thinking he'd already done that about four months ago. "I take care of myself."

"Did you come all the way from Montana?"

"Um, yes. I drove here. Thirty-one hours. I took breaks. I've been driving on and off for two days."

"You should have called me, and I would have come to you."

"Well, I didn't have your number. And I was on my way to Chicago, anyway." And taken an approximately fifteen-hour detour, but never mind that.

"I would have come to you in Chicago." He dragged another hand through his close-cropped hair.

Probably force of habit from when it was wavy and long. She missed his gorgeous dark hair and recalled running her fingers through it.

"Honestly? I wasn't sure if you'd remember me."

His neck jerked back as if she'd slapped him. "Of *course*, I remember you."

But the way he'd moved that night, the way he'd looked, so confident in his own skin, she thought maybe he hooked up with random women often. *She* didn't hook up at all. Adam was something of a recluse according to everyone she'd talked to when she'd first started looking for him after confirming the pregnancy. No one ever saw him with a woman.

He didn't have many friends and seemed to do nothing but work.

"Why didn't you find me sooner? I've been in Marion until recently."

"I know, and I'm sorry. I just wanted to get past that first trimester. This could have gone another way, and in that case, you would have never known."

He narrowed his eyes. "You weren't going to tell me at all, were you?"

Bingo. He knew.

"Um, well… Adam, you seemed kind of lost, you know? Haunted." *Still pining away for the woman in the photo she'd seen.* "I didn't want to bring you any more trouble. But in the end, I know it was the right thing to do." *And Grace talked me into it.* "Like I said, you don't need to do anything. I just wanted you to know."

"Hey, guys!" A pretty and perky blonde came up to their booth, holding the hand of a man who looked like he'd stepped out of the pages of *GQ* magazine. She looked expectantly at Stacy. "I'm Ava Long. And this is Max Del Toro, my fiancé. We just put up the Christmas tree today. Welcome to Charming!"

Wow. It was as if someone had just charged her batteries. Or maybe she was like the Energizer Bunny. Stacy was ready for a nap just listening to her talk. Then again, she'd been exhausted lately and all the hours driving hadn't helped.

"Ava, Max, this is my friend Stacy Hartsell," Adam

said. "Max is one of my best friends. I've known him for over ten years."

Max offered his hand. "Nice to meet you."

"Same," Stacy said, shaking Max's hand. "I knew Adam…when he lived in Montana."

"How long are you staying?" Ava asked.

"I'm just passing through on my way to Chicago."

"Maybe you should stay tonight," Adam offered. "Driving that many hours would make anyone tired."

"Oh, I plan to take a rest," Stacy said. "I need to frequently nap these days."

"Stacy is pregnant," Adam said.

"Congratulations," Max said.

"That's amazing. What a great Christmas present," Ava said.

Then Max and Ava looked from Stacy to Adam, and back at each other. They'd put it all together.

"Well, we should go and leave these two to eat their lunch." Max put his arm around Ava.

"Yes," Ava said. "There's that thing…we need to… Bye!"

With that, they hustled away, arm in arm.

"Cute couple. I think they suspect this is your baby," Stacy said, wishing he hadn't said anything. "You didn't have to tell them. Most people think I'm fat."

"Why? They'll find out sooner or later. And both are fairly bright people." Adam studied her.

Now *she* drummed her fingers on the table.

"Aren't you going to eat?" He pointed to the burger.

"You're still not hungry?"

He shook his head.

It made sense that it might take him a while to recover from the shock of her news. He'd likely lost his appetite.

"Okay, then."

She bit into the burger, which was juicy, and…oh, Lord, incredible. Though she mostly refrained from eating red meat as a rule, since the pregnancy, she'd been craving it. She didn't speak for several minutes, didn't even look at Adam, because this burger was an experience for all five senses. It had a charbroiled taste and the bun was soft enough to be homemade. And the sauce was both creamy and delicious.

When she glanced up between bites, Adam was smiling at her. He had a nice one-dimple smile. Something else she hadn't forgotten about him.

"Hey, Debbie," he called out to the waitress. "Bring a glass of milk, would ya?"

When she set down the glass in front of Adam, he slid it over to her as well. "Hope you're not lactose intolerant."

"Thanks." She took a sip of milk and wiped her mouth. "Adam, you claimed you were single that night, but I sure hope I'm not going to make someone else's life complicated, too."

"Still single." He cleared his throat. "You?"

"Yes, sure. It's not a great time to start up a relationship." She paused, wondering how to phrase the next question. "Don't you want a paternity test?"

Both Grace and Stacy's mother had prepped her for this. They'd assumed any man in this situation would ask for one. Stacy had steeled herself for the question, vowing not to be offended.

Adam drew his eyebrows together. "Why? Could the baby belong to someone else?"

"Well, no. Not possible at all, but…you're just taking my word for this."

"Maybe so, but I don't sleep with people that I don't trust."

Oh. O-kay. "Well, gosh, thank you."

"Besides, why would you lie, when you're obviously trying to get rid of me?" He leaned back and stretched his long arms. "And, I'm guessing you already realize I don't have much money."

"I…assumed. Yes."

"So why would you lie?"

"I wouldn't, but, I don't know, maybe some woman who thought she could get you to settle down with her…"

He smirked. "That's not you. I get it. You have this handled. Don't need me."

Great. That made guilt spike through her. "It's just… I mean, of course, you can be involved if you'd like."

"Thanks."

"We could work something out. I'll send you copies of the ultrasounds. Keep you updated, maybe via email, or text."

"Okay."

"But... I hope you understand if I don't want you in the delivery room."

She tried not to look at him but failed. He wasn't smiling, was simply quietly listening. Some men might joke about how they'd already seen her hoo-ha. He had, but she'd rather not have him as an observer as she pushed an eight-pounder out of it. Even *she* didn't want to see that. So Adam wasn't the type for crude jokes. Confirmed. However, he didn't agree or disagree, making her a little...jumpy.

"Well, I guess I'll be on my way to find a hotel room. I'm sure Houston will have more availability." She finished the rest of her hamburger in silence then reached for one last drink of milk.

"You can stay with me tonight."

She nearly choked. "That's...really okay. I have a long drive ahead of me."

"It seems ridiculous to spend the money when I have a place for you to stay. And I'm the father of your baby. I'm not going to hurt you."

"Oh, no. I know that." Had he been a serial killer he would have had his chance with her four months ago.

"It will give us just a little more time to get to know each other before you leave. We're going to be parents."

The thought terrified her. It was why she'd wanted to ignore Grace's well-intentioned advice. This could get complicated. She'd hoped Adam would be frightened enough by the news to deny he could possibly be the father. Or to thank her for letting him know and send her on her merry way. But what if Adam followed her to Chicago to be more involved? She didn't look forward to co-parenting with someone she didn't even know.

Even if, clearly, Adam did seem to be a good guy who wanted to do the right thing. It was selfish, sure, but from the moment she'd decided to become a mother, she'd wanted control over everything. Just like her mother had with her. It would be difficult, of course, but she had resources. Support. Doing this on her own would mean she wouldn't be forced to consult with someone over trips, health-care decisions, education, holidays. If she included Adam, it would be like starting off as a divorced couple, and co-parenting. Then again, doing this without the father's support also meant no economic input. Not the ideal situation.

At one time in her life, she'd imagined doing this in the right order. Falling in love, getting married, having children, raising them together. Happily ever after. Never, ever getting a divorce. The end.

"I have to get back to work," Adam said. "My break is over. But here's the key to my place. You take the bedroom tonight and I'll be in the spare room. Take a shower, relax, nap, whatever you'd like. Make yourself at home. We can talk more later."

He stood and walked to the bar, moving as she remembered. Like a panther. He grabbed some paper and a pen from the bartender. Heads together, they seemed to be consulting with each other.

When Adam returned, he'd written down the address with directions. "You can't get lost in Charming."

She decided to spare him the details of the five times she'd taken a wrong turn on the way to Charming. Special skill of hers. Digging in her purse, she came out with her wallet. "How much do I owe you for lunch?"

"That's on the house," he said, bracing both hands on the table. "It's good to see you, Stacy."

That almost sounded as though he'd missed her, which, of course, he had not. If he'd wanted to find her after that night, he could have. Then again, she'd been the one to sneak out and leave him a note:

This was fun, but please don't contact me again.

Oh, but those eyes…so warm. So inviting. She swallowed hard.

I'm not doing this.

I'm not kidding myself.

He's hung up on someone else.

He feels responsible for me and that's all.

"Um, are you sure this is okay? I'm not going to run in to anyone who *also* has a key?"

He cocked his head and met her eyes. "No."

"Okay, thanks. I appreciate this, but I'm leaving first thing in the morning."

Chapter Three

Adam finished his shift as if moving through a room filled with thick molasses. He got orders wrong and forgot to set timers. Worked at roughly the pace of a snail on Xanax. Thankfully, Brian covered for him.

"You okay, boss?"

"Uh, yeah. Yeah. Thanks. I'm…good."

No, he wasn't *good*. A more appropriate word would be *stunned*. What would Brian say if Adam answered, "No, I'm not okay. I'm shocked. Dismayed. Astonished."

Thesaurus, anyone?

His life had changed in two *minutes*. He would be a father. A *father*. Someone's "daddy." And Stacy… damn, she still looked stunning. Pregnancy agreed with her. The weight was all in her belly, and somehow, in her *breasts*, which strained against her long-sleeved sweater. He recalled she had an amazing set, but now they were decidedly...larger. She'd arrived dressed in Montana winter clothes, obviously not prepared for a Gulf Coast kind of winter. And driven for thirty-one hours!

This worried him. She'd likely driven through some snow and sleet. Did she always make such dangerous choices? He trusted her, but what did he really know about Stacy? For one thing, she took risks. For months, he'd noticed her coming into the only bar in Marion. Always alone. Ordered one beer and sipped it while she read a book. Got hit on approximately once an hour. Not by him. He never approached anyone, choosing to play pool with the guys, unwind and relax.

But he wasn't jaded enough to ignore *her*. Long, dark, straight hair, big eyes. That amazing mouth, with a full upper lip slightly bigger than the lower one. Long legs, perky breasts, curvy butt. The men talked about her often.

"Cold fish," one had said.

"Barracuda," another had added.

"Turned me down flat. Must be a lesbian."

Then, one night, she'd sat next to him at the bar as he nursed his drink. Ordered a beer and opened her book.

"Hey, baby, can I buy you a beer?" a local had asked her within two minutes.

She looked up from her book and pointed to her nearly full glass. "No thanks."

He was not discouraged. "Are you a writer? The guys say you're a writer. What kind?"

The smile she gave him transformed her face from simply gorgeous to mischievous.

"I kill people in my books. Sometimes I have to do a lot of research to find the best way to get rid of a body while leaving little evidence of a crime."

"Oh, hey there, look at the time. Nice chattin' with ya. 'Bye!"

Adam chuckled as he watched the man go. "That one scares easily."

She turned to him. "I can't blame him. What, it doesn't scare you that I know how to get rid of a body without leaving any evidence?"

"Nah, but maybe because I also know how. And that it's not *entirely* possible."

She blinked. "What's not entirely possible?"

"Not leaving any evidence."

"Right. DNA, for instance." She tossed back her long hair. "A tough one. I could never get away with murder. My hair alone would convict me."

He nodded, then held up his beer in a mock toast to her amazing hair.

She closed her book. "Are *you* a writer?"

"Not me, no. Just a soldier."

It was a simple enough answer for most. He didn't distinguish between the Army—technically, the branch of the service that included soldiers—and the Navy. Not with civilians.

She took a pull of her beer and studied him from hooded lids. "I thought you were a cowboy."

"For now, I am. But more like a goat boy, if that's even a thing."

"Sorry, doesn't sound nearly as sexy."

He met her gaze, which held the hint of another naughty smile. She was *beautiful*. Bright eyes framed by long lashes, those irises shimmering with humor and intelligence. He couldn't look away. He'd been mesmerized. That night, for a few hours, he'd forgotten Mandy ever existed, which later brought about a fresh new wave of guilt. That might have been the reason he'd never tried to find Stacy even after the kiss-off note she'd left him. Clearly, one night was all he'd deserved.

But for that one incredible night, he'd been changed. He hadn't been lost. Not lonely. No longer grieving.

They spent the rest of the night playing pool and talking. He'd told her all about the goat farm where he worked. She told him about the first book she'd had published, a thriller, and the sequel she was struggling to finish. With the ability to work from anywhere, she'd decided to slowly make her way across the United States. Stacy was originally from Chicago, one place he'd actually never been.

For two strangers who'd started off the night talking about hiding evidence of a crime, neither one of them had any hesitation at the end of the evening. They'd spent the night together in his cabin. The connection, the trust between them, made everything else fade to black. Those memories remained the single most erotic ones of his life. But the next morning she'd been gone, leaving him a note which said she thought it best if they didn't see each other again. Made it too easy for Adam to walk away.

He'd thought about her often, when the guilt abated enough to allow him. In his fantasies, he'd walk into a room where he could be alone with her. Once in a while, he indulged in a fantasy that he'd met Stacy years ago, before he was ruined. When he'd had something to offer.

Now she was here, in Charming, pregnant with *his* baby. The result of failed birth control—damn useless condom. But he shouldn't feel this rush of anticipation. He shouldn't be happy about this mess. His life would change yet again and not likely for the better.

"See you tomorrow," Brian said, snapping Adam out of his fog.

He'd have to tell Cole and Max about Stacy, but not until he'd wrapped his own mind around his new reality. There was a shortage of rentals in Charming, so when Ava had moved in with Max, Adam moved out. And right into Ava's former rental. It was a small place with two bedrooms, one so small that Ava had used it as a walk-in closet. Adam planned to use it as a weight room eventually. Tonight, he'd sleep on the floor in there, or on the living-room couch.

Susannah Ferguson, his senior-citizen neighbor, was outside when he arrived home after his shift. Her little poodle, who went by the ridiculous name of Doodle, yipped and yapped in her arms, determined to terrify Adam.

"Hey, Mrs. Ferguson. Everything okay?"

"I should ask you that, sugar. There's a strange woman in your house." She nudged her chin. "Guess it takes all kinds."

"It's all right, I gave her the key."

"Oh." Her eyebrows went up. "Is that your sister?"

"No, not my sister."

He could see why she might think so. They both had dark hair about the same shade, but Stacy was the furthest thing from a sister that she could possibly be. Adam was still getting used to living this close to a nosy neighbor. For months, he'd lived in a cabin on the farm, and his main company had been the goats. They never asked him any personal questions.

"She's a friend of mine from Montana. Visiting."

"Well, that's all right then. Good for you. I'm glad you have a nice friend."

"Thanks for keeping an eye on the place." He had nothing worth stealing, but Mrs. Ferguson meant well.

"You're welcome." Susannah waved and crossed the shared lawn to her house.

He opened the door to find Stacy soundly asleep on the couch. She hadn't taken the bed he'd offered. Maybe that meant she wouldn't even stay the night. He had to get her to stay at least tonight. Reluctant to wake her by cooking her dinner, he took a shower and wiped away the grime of the grill.

Ava's presence was still a strong one in this house, and she'd left some of her furniture since she and Max didn't need two of everything. Adam didn't need much. A bed, a TV, a lamp. But now he tried to picture this small home filled with a *crib* and a high chair. Whatever else babies needed. What was *he* going to do with a baby? He couldn't just walk away, but he needed some time to think this through. Figure out a solution. Surely, he had something he could offer Stacy and their child.

Max and Cole had been generous with his salary. They'd also offered him a chance to buy in to the bar. That required a commitment on his part, and an investment. He hadn't given them an answer yet. Investing in the bar would require filing for the insurance policy that Mandy had left for him. For the first time, he considered it. He might not feel worthy, but his baby had done nothing wrong. He or she hadn't asked to be born to a father who didn't have his act together.

Should he offer marriage to Stacy? Adam could hear his Portuguese father's voice all the way from El Paso: "*Mijo*, do the right thing. Take care of her. Offer marriage."

But Stacy wouldn't go for it. Not a marriage out of convenience or honor. Certainly not when he didn't love her. When she didn't love him. And she'd stressed her independence from the night they'd met. Clearly, that hadn't changed. She thought she could raise *their* child on her own. Had already made her plans. Actually, he should consider himself fortunate she'd bothered to tell him at all. A flash of anger spiked through him. Call it a delayed reaction. This was his child, too.

He shut off the shower and toweled himself dry. Stacy's plans would have to be reconsidered in light of everything he'd learned. She couldn't just walk away from him. After wrapping the towel around his waist, he opened the door and let the steam waft out.

Stacy stood at the end of the hallway, rubbing her eyes.

"Hey. Glad you're awake. We need to talk."

Stacy blinked and tried not to stare at Adam's sculpted chest and abs. She'd seen him naked before, *all* of him, but…not like this. Not in the clear light of day, the sunlight filtering through the window making him shimmer and shine like the statue of a Greek god. And wet, his skin damp and fresh, a towel draped low on his hips. His jaw was tight, his mouth rigid. She sensed the energy of anger and hostility shooting off him in waves. Uh-oh.

"Um, sure. Let's talk. But I just woke up, so give me a minute."

"I'll get dressed." He walked into the bedroom and shut the door.

Shut the door to the bedroom with a bed she'd refused to sleep in once she'd seen the room. Feminine touches were everywhere, which meant that Adam had lived here with a woman. Or still did. He'd lied. Maybe he and his wife or significant other were separated, and he simply called himself "single." What did she know? Maybe they'd been separated until he moved back to Texas. She didn't think he'd take the chance on giving her a key if the other woman was still around. But she could be on a trip. Oh, Lord! And she was pregnant with this man's baby. This woman was going to kill Stacy.

This is what you get for sleeping with someone you don't know.

Those were her mother's words, ringing in her ears, but they were true, nonetheless. Stacy had fooled herself the night she'd gone home with him. She'd believed they had started something real. Adam had given her everything. He's *listened* to her, not just gone through the motions, hoping she'd sleep with him. She knew what that looked like. It wasn't even his idea to sleep together. *What a find*, Stacy had thought then. Out here in the boondocks, the one attractive and interesting man in the world not on the make.

But the next morning, she'd seen the framed photo. A *wedding* photo. Adam, handsome in a black tux with a short blond woman who radiated joy. Beautiful, her smile sweet and saintly.

The woman he loves.

Ladies and gentlemen, in this corner, the woman he screws; in that corner, the woman he adores. The next morning, she'd written him a quick note suggesting they never see each other again and left before he woke. Considered him a mistake and a learning experience. Hoo, boy. What was that old quote about some mistakes being irreversible?

"But you're not a mistake," she whispered, hand low on her abdomen. "You're mine."

Stacy would have to call her mother soon and update her on the drive, or she'd panic further. There were already two missed calls, one when she'd been napping. But now was not the time. She could hear Adam in the bedroom, slamming around in there. Well. This should be fun. He might as well find out right now that the mother of his child was a tough woman who wouldn't fold or deviate from her plans just because a guy was sulking.

She forced herself to sit on the couch and wait, ignoring that she was already hungry again. Adam came out dressed in jeans and an old, worn Navy T-shirt. She thought he'd been in the Army, a soldier. Did it belong to him, or his absent wife or girlfriend?

He stopped right in front of her. "Are you hungry?"

Darn mind reader. "Yes, but let's talk first. I don't think I'll lose my appetite, no matter what you have to say."

He quirked an eyebrow. "What does *that* mean?"

"You might as well tell me about the woman who obviously lived here until recently. You lied to me. You're *not* single. I just want to know what my odds are of getting out of this day without someone keying my car."

"I didn't lie. I'm single. Have been for years. I live alone."

"Stop *lying*! Those are matching shams on your bed. Shams! Do you think I'm stupid?"

He scowled. "What the hell are shams?"

"They're those pretty large pillow covers that your woman picked out. Very feminine. Don't even *try* and tell me that a woman doesn't live here. Her touches are everywhere."

He scrubbed a hand down his face.

Aha! Busted.

"A woman lived here very recently, and you've met her. Ava Long, my buddy Max's fiancée. She moved in with Max, and I moved out of Max's, where I'd been staying. She hasn't even moved all of her stuff out, and sorry if I haven't had time to 'redecorate.'" He held up air quotes with his smirk.

Now she felt stupid. She'd been so certain. Blame it on baby brain.

"Okay, you're single." She cleared her throat. "I believe you. Glad we cleared that up. What did you want to talk about?"

He sat on the couch. "I want to be an involved father. I have rights and I want visitation. I don't want to be relegated just to holidays and summers. I want all in. This is my baby, too."

She swallowed hard, her future life flashing before her eyes, one of constant compromises, and every other weekend spent away from her baby.

Adam kept talking. "I know you've already made all your plans and I'm sorry to break them."

"I knew this was too good to be true." She rubbed her thighs with her palms, suddenly filled with unspent nervous energy. "You were so nice. *So* understanding."

"I'm still nice and understanding."

"But you want to change everything."

"Did you really expect me not to want to have anything to do with my baby?" He waited a beat. "Don't answer that. That's exactly what you thought."

"When we met, you were working on a goat farm in the middle of nowhere. Forgive me if I didn't think you'd be interested in becoming a family man. Besides, I thought—"

"What?"

That you were still in love with someone else.

"Never mind."

Considering everything, she didn't see the point in asking why she'd seen only one photo in the living room of his cabin: his wedding photo. She didn't see the photo anywhere now, not in the bedroom or in the living room, but there was still time. Adam said he'd just moved in.

"What about health insurance? You're a writer. Doesn't that mean you're self-employed?"

"Yes. It's not great insurance, but, yes, I have it."

Her insurance plan, purchased through the guild, would cover most everything, though with incredibly high deductibles and co-pays. But with her mother's help, Stacy could cut corners and pay the enormous medical deductibles she'd face.

"I have good insurance through the VA."

"That will come in handy for our child after she's born. I appreciate that."

"It can help you, too."

"I don't see how. They have strict rules about that sort of thing."

"Then, let's get married."

Chapter Four

Stacy couldn't speak. Too busy trying to breathe. For a writer, this was one hell of a plot twist. She stared at Adam, jaw gaping, and wondered when he'd realize what a terrible idea he'd proposed. Ha! Proposed. No, he hadn't *proposed*. That would be the romantic way, and Lord knew they weren't in that place.

Suggested. He'd suggested they get married. He *looked* like a bright man. How on earth could he...?

"Say something."

Stacy wet her parched lips. Though she hadn't been sick in over a month, that old twisty bile threatened to make a reappearance. She pushed it back down and took a deep breath. Still couldn't get a word out.

Adam filled the silence. "If we get married, all your prenatal visits, the birth and delivery, that will all be covered."

Nope, he wasn't stupid. Bright as they came. What he suggested made sense for someone who didn't have any pride. Or any resources of her own. She had yet to come up with words. Kind of embarrassing for a writer.

"Thank you, but no."

"Don't you at least want to think about it? I mean, this could be an answer to some of your problems."

"Jumping off a bridge is also an answer but I'm not going to do that, either."

He flinched.

Oh, right. She'd just said she'd rather jump off a bridge than marry him. Now *she* scrubbed a hand down her face. Sometimes she forgot to keep the hyperbole in her books.

"I...just... Listen, that's super sweet and I appreciate it. Obviously, I'd rather marry you than jump off a bridge. I mean, I'm not going to do either."

Now he didn't speak, simply studied her in silence, as if he was wondering if she could be trusted to host his spawn.

Stacy rubbed her hands on her thighs. "You don't love me, and I don't love you. We shouldn't get married. Okay?"

"Whether we love each other or not isn't the issue.

We're having a child together, like it or not. We don't have to sleep together. Just live as roommates. There's a VA hospital in Houston about twenty minutes away."

"You want me to stay *here*?"

"Why not? I've got a house, and you're already here. No more driving. After the baby comes, well, we can reconsider. Get a divorce and co-parent. Obviously, we'll have to live close by each other. I would consider moving to Chicago."

This was just too much. She needed a sandwich. Another nap. She had to talk to her mother.

"Adam, if you're so single, why did you have a framed photo of your wedding day on display?" The question was out of her mouth before she would rethink.

"What?"

"The photo in your living-room bookcase. I couldn't miss it the morning after we...you know. I don't know too many men who keep a photo of their wedding day for all to see if they're not still married."

He blinked. "I'm sorry you saw that, but you don't have to worry. I've been single for years. She's no longer in the picture."

Notice how he doesn't say "ex-wife." Single for years, but still hung up on her.

"Okay, well, wow. I'm so sorry. That must be tough. I'm sure your heart was broken."

Not denying it, he narrowed his eyes. "What does that have to do with us?"

"I think I should know who you are, don't you?"

"Obviously. We'll have about six months to get to know each other. How's that?"

She had to be light-headed from low blood sugar because she was actually considering this ridiculous arrangement. Her mother would want to have her committed, but Grace would probably write it into her next "marriage of convenience" book. Stacy had just given her new material.

"Um...could I please have something to eat?"

He jumped up. "Yeah. Of course."

Within minutes, she had a sandwich in front of her, and a glass of milk. Cookies. The thin slices of turkey were delicious, with fresh sprouts, cucumber and tomato slices on a nutty grain bread. So her baby's daddy was a good cook, and a goat farmer. Some kind of a soldier. To her, this meant he hadn't been able to hold down a job for long since his military service.

He might have some PTSD and certainly residual grief over his ex-wife. A divorce made sense. So many marriages didn't survive long separations due to deployments. Unless she'd *died*. Stacy didn't want to ask him and bring up something even more difficult than what they were already handling. But keeping their wedding photo... He wasn't over her, however long it had been. If she'd died, that would make sense, too.

He couldn't be ready for any of this, and yet he was trying. This was...kind. She felt her heart split and her eyes water. The pregnancy hormones had her far more emotional than was normal for her.

She stood. "Thank you for the meal. I think I'm... I need to call my mother. Maybe lie down for a little. Do you mind?"

In a few long strides, he was by the bedroom door down the short hallway, holding it open for her. "Go ahead. And let me know if you need anything, okay?"

She brushed by him, his fresh, clean smell stirring something deep in her belly. If she went through with this insanity, she couldn't allow herself to fall in love with him. Already, she saw how easy that would be. Similar to the night they'd met when she'd thought—she'd *known*—there was something real between them. A connection. But she'd been wrong, hadn't she, because it had been entirely one-sided. To him, it was only sex. Exactly the expectation most people would have from a random hookup. She couldn't even blame him, so hadn't asked for anything more, especially after the photo.

Her mother picked up on the second ring. "How far are you? Drive carefully, we're expecting some terrible weather. I'll hold dinner if you're close."

"No. Don't wait. It's going to be a while."

"*Now* what?"

"I took a little detour. I'm in Texas. The Gulf Coast, to be precise."

"That's quite a detour. I knew it was a bad idea for you to drive. What on earth are you doing there?"

Making a huge mistake? Doing the right thing? Both were likely true. And then Stacy told her mother everything. How Grace found Adam in Charming, and Stacy drove down to give him the news in person.

"What did he say? Did he ask for a paternity test?" Mom's tone was laced with disgust for the entire male species.

She had decades of experience to back her up.

"He believes me."

Stacy *should* be believed. She wasn't the type to be with more than one man per, um, let's see… decade? Slight exaggeration. Her last serious relationship, with Daniel, lasted five years. She'd been that soft place for him to fall after a painful divorce.

Mom didn't think it possible that a man Stacy had been with only once would believe no one else could be the father given the circumstances. Yes, she'd shared those circumstances with her mother. Sometimes, Stacy wished she and Mom had more boundaries. But they'd practically grown up together, the two of them, like best friends. Her mother had been a single mom by the time she turned twenty-two. They'd lived with her maternal grandmother, all three of them close, while Mom put herself through nursing school.

"Okay, well, now you've done the right thing. Hope you feel good about this. When can I expect you?"

It went against her modus operandi, but Stacy threw up a boundary from the safety of long dis-

tance. Her mother couldn't read her face in that un-
canny way she had.

"I'm going to stay the night because of all the
driving. I took breaks, but it was still exhausting."

"That sounds wise. I'd worry about you driving
all night in bad weather."

But south Texas meant Stacy had slipped straight
into summer, bypassing winter and spring. It was
warm and lovely, especially after Montana.

She wouldn't tell her mother about Adam's suggestion that they get married. Besides, Stacy was simply
considering this, and hadn't made a decision. It would
be smart to let him help with the medical expenses.
She wouldn't trick herself with any of the rest. Separate beds, separate bank accounts. Separate lives.

That's the only way this would work. Then, after
her baby girl was born, she'd move to Chicago to live
with Mom, who would help babysit so Stacy could
meet her deadlines. If Adam wanted to follow her
and give up his job here, that would be up to him.

But she didn't think he'd do that. Adam was on a
guilt trip. Once she allowed him to contribute in some
way, that sense of responsibility would be relieved.
Maybe he'd be a part-time, long-distance father,
though the idea of sending her child back to Charming for summers was too painful to contemplate.

"You idiot," Adam muttered to himself as he
wiped the kitchen counter and put away the sandwich fixings.

Stacy had seen the framed wedding photo. He would have put it away, but he'd hardly been prepared for that crazy night with her. The photo reminded him, every time he looked at it, that despite being cash-strapped some days, he didn't have a right to the life-insurance money from Mandy. He'd never filed for the benefits. Adam didn't want or deserve the money. He'd failed his wife. His last words to her…well, he still couldn't forgive himself. But now, maybe his future child could have the money. He'd at least have something to give. Something to contribute. Soon, he'd make a call to the insurance company and start the process.

Now he understood the note Stacy had left him and what changed between them. Because even though he understood that they were likely just a one-night stand, Adam felt more for Stacy than he'd intended to. He wasn't the kind of man built for one-night stands. He'd wanted to see her again, wanted to try again with a woman for the first time in a long while. But when she'd made her feelings clear, he chose the easy way out. He didn't have to see her again, much as he might have wanted to. He didn't deserve her, either. It was easier not to risk feeling anything deeply again. Easier for him to stay away.

But now, he realized that without meaning to, he'd gravely insulted the mother of his child. Not just once, but twice, if he wanted to count the proposal. First the wedding photo, now the suggestion that he would take pity on her by offering marriage. At his suggestion, all the color had drained out of her face.

Sure, maybe it was stupid to bring up marriage this soon, but with the timeline she'd given him he didn't have the luxury of waiting. They were going to be parents and getting married for the health insurance was a logical decision. A wise one. There didn't have to be any emotions involved. Even if there already were, at least on his part.

Stacy was fiercely independent, tough and a smart-ass. And in the bedroom? A wild woman. There didn't seem to be a sweet level to her, but he'd guess that he didn't exactly bring it out. She would be a good mother, of that he felt certain. Just the way she touched her belly protectively. And the fact that she'd come all the way to Charming to tell him he'd be a father told him the rest. She wanted to do the right thing.

So Adam would sleep in the spare bedroom. He could make this work. All he required was Stacy's cooperation. But he'd heard her end of the conversation with her mother, and it didn't sound too promising for him.

Yes, I told him.

Sure, I'll start driving early in the morning.

No, I'm fine. Yes. Please, don't worry.

A few minutes later, she came out of the bedroom, with a red nose and red-rimmed eyes. Damn it.

"You okay?"

She sniffed and wiped her nose with a tissue. "It's

an emotional time. Hormones raging. This isn't the norm for me. I haven't cried this much since *Next Year in Havana*."

Maybe because of his blank expression, she shrugged. "It's a book."

"Listen, I may have come on too strong suggesting marriage."

"You think?" She smiled, the same wicked one she'd given him the night they'd met.

He had a feeling she did not know the effect it had on men. Her smile enticed a man to think about all manner of randy fantasies. She'd fulfilled every one of them that night. Even now, pregnant and about as off-limits as a woman could get for him, he ached to touch her again. To press her into the mattress and feel her wrap those long legs around his back one more time.

"I'll consider your offer, I promise, but I'll do it from Chicago."

He felt her slipping through his fingers, taking everything with her. Any chance of living again.

Loving again.

"What about a week?"

"For...?"

"Give me a week and consider my proposal."

"Adam, please, that wasn't a *proposal*."

"Sorry, I meant my suggestion. My offer."

She studied him steadily, those blue eyes shimmering. "The marriage of convenience."

"Look, I know you could do a lot better than me.

But I'm asking you to think about this. I will take care of you. You won't need anything. Just give me the week. That's all I'm asking for."

She chewed on her lower lip. "A week."

"A week to fully *consider* this, at least."

"I know you're trying to be kind, but I have some pride. I didn't mean for you to feel this obligated to me...to us."

A surge of unexplainable tenderness hit him like a rogue wave. "I remember. You're fully capable on your own, but I want at least a real chance to state my case."

"And at the end of a week, you'll accept my answer?"

"I promise you, I will. No matter what it is."

"All right, a week." She crossed her arms. "And no foolin' around, mister. Separate rooms. Separate beds."

"You're pregnant! Of course, no foolin' around."

She quirked an eyebrow. "This may come as a shock to you, but pregnant women can and do have sex. Not that anyone *wants* to have sex with them."

With that, she turned and padded back to the bedroom, softly closing the door behind her.

I wouldn't bet on it, sweetheart.

He supposed that made him a sick man, because he couldn't stop thinking about just that.

Chapter Five

When Stacy woke the next morning, she thought she might have imagined yesterday. But this was real. Everything from the silky sheets she now stretched on to the pillow sham she'd drooled on. She pulled the blanket over her face, wanting to hide, wishing she didn't have to make yet another monumental decision in the space of a week. In the last four months, she'd made more life-changing decisions than she'd made over the previous ten years. Leave it to Adam to throw yet another one her way.

She didn't feel capable of making this big of a decision. Marriage to a man she barely knew, even if he'd made a good case for it. She would love to have great health insurance paid for by the United

States government. Stacy wasn't a true romantic, so she didn't need flowers, candy, dinner by candlelight and declarations of undying love. Above all else, she was practical to a fault, and marriage to Adam unfortunately made a lot of sense.

But she absolutely refused to make this decision before the week was up. Just as with her deadlines, Stacy would take every day given to her before turning in her manuscript. Always on time, but not an hour earlier. She might even see pushing this decision longer than a week, if Adam was kind enough to grant her an extension on her deadline. Um, decision, she meant.

What would she tell her mother? *Nothing.* Stacy would make something up because she'd been telling her mother stories from the time she was a child. Mom had called them *lies*, and then later, fanciful creations and tall tales. Stacy preferred to call them creative diversions. Eventually she did tell her mother the truth, evidenced by her confession about how she'd become pregnant in the first place. Not a proud moment.

She rolled out of bed and peered out the blinds on the window. Rays of bright sunshine spilled over the Texas day. Strange weather for the holiday season. Back in Montana, she hadn't seen the sun in weeks. No wonder Adam had moved here, even if for a job as a cook in a bar and grill. The Salty Dog had been bustling yesterday, filled with customers. For someone used to a solitary life working on a goat farm, this had to be quite the change for him, too.

Well, the first thing she'd have to do is buy some new clothes. She wouldn't last a week in this weather before tearing off all her clothes and shocking Adam. She normally ran cold, but the occasional hot flash was among all the wonderful things pregnancy hormones had done to her body. Her spring and summer clothes were in one of the first boxes she'd shipped to Chicago, realizing she wouldn't need them for a while. Now she had nothing but sweaters and her trusty yoga pants with a lot of stretch.

She sat on the edge of her bed and wondered whether she should take a shower first, or call her mother, or take another look at her editor's notes for the current manuscript. No slouch in the procrastination department, Stacy decided to take a shower. She'd slept in her underwear, having not so much as a T-shirt in her luggage. But because she was sharing the house with a guy, even if he was the father of her baby, she would have to get dressed to walk to the *bathroom*.

Opening the door to the bedroom, she peeked outside. Adam was already moving around in the kitchen. She found him bent over a skillet frying potatoes and eggs, wearing a backward-facing baseball cap.

What is this madness?

If he wanted to get married, he should have just mentioned that he cooked at home, too.

"You *work* as a cook and you also cook at home? I thought that wasn't allowed."

He glanced up but his mouth didn't so much as twitch. "You want some of these eggs and potatoes?"

"Well, okay. You twisted my arm. If you insist." She took a seat on a stool near the counter of the small kitchen.

"I have to work a shift today, but feel free to take a shower and make yourself at home." He expertly plated the meal and set it in front of her.

"Until yesterday, I didn't know you were a professional cook. I thought you were a cowboy and a soldier."

"There's a lot you don't know about me."

Touché, cowboy, touché.

"Even if I'm only going to be here for a week, I'll need to buy a few lighter clothes. I might look funny walking around in my parka." She took a bite. Delicious. The scrambled eggs were moist and the potatoes crispy and warm. Maybe she should have proposed to *him*.

"Same thing happened to me. I walked down the boardwalk when I first arrived and got a few strange looks." He set a chilled glass of orange juice in front of her. "I'll have Ava or Valerie let you know what the best places are to buy clothes around here."

She'd met Ava and Max yesterday. "Who's Valerie?"

"Valerie is my buddy Cole Kinsella's fiancée. He's the bartender and part owner of the Salty Dog. Max is the other owner."

"Hmm. That explains why you're suddenly working as a cook."

"I've worked as a cook before, straight out of the military. Max found himself in a bind. He'd fired his head cook and wanted to bring me in. Honestly, he's been wanting to bring me in since they took over the place. I just wasn't interested."

"Loved Montana too much?"

"I was *comfortable* on the farm." He took a bite of egg straight out the pan and studied her. "Until I met you."

"I tend to have that effect on people. Men meet me, and suddenly get a hankering to see the rest of the country." She shoveled in another bite. "I think it's because I write thrillers."

"That's not it. At the bar, men were uncomfortable around you because you were so beautiful."

"They were uncomfortable because I sat at the bar and read a book. I'm not great with the chitchat."

"You did fine with me."

"Well, that's not the norm."

"Me, neither." He met her eyes. "*You* were not the norm for me. After that night, I wanted to see you again."

She froze, her fork halfway to her mouth. "I hope you understand why I didn't think that was a good idea."

"I do *now*." Lowering his gaze to her nearly empty plate, he served her more potatoes. "I'm sorry, too."

"You don't have to apologize. You're single and I

believe you now. But being single and still being in love with someone are two different things."

"No. That's not the issue. It's—"

She held up a palm, hating that she'd put him on the spot. "Please. You really *don't* need to explain."

"I feel like I do."

"Because you're a good guy, you knocked me up, and I *found* you." She snapped her fingers.

This time, his mouth twitched at the corners. "Hey, I wanted to see you again, but the note you left made it clear you didn't return the favor."

"Because I saw the photo."

"That was a mistake."

"Having the photo, or letting me to see it?"

He leaned his back against the counter, arms crossed. "Both."

"It's okay. I don't want to put you on the spot anymore. Let's just say that we've moved on." She made a sweeping motion with her hands.

"I don't think that's enough. You need to know."

He was right, of course. Stacy had inserted herself into this triangle, an unwilling and unknowing participant. She should know what she'd be up against. Already strong suspicions had formed that this woman he clearly adored might no longer be among the living. Stacy would hate that for Adam, but it could explain hanging on to the wedding photo.

The reverence. The bittersweet memories.

"Are you a widower?"

Maybe if *she* said the words, maybe if she was

the first to say them out loud, they wouldn't be as hard to hear.

Adam slowly nodded.

"Oh, Adam, I'm so sorry."

He lowered his head and studied the floor. "It's okay. It was a while ago."

Stacy wasn't sure if that made this better, or worse. And clearly, he was far from okay. "How long ago?"

"About four years."

Poor Adam.

"Not that long ago." A short enough time to still display a wedding photo. "How did it happen?"

"An IED explosion in Kandahar."

"She was a soldier, too?"

"No, a doctor. She was with Doctors Without Borders, at a bad time for civilians to be in the area."

"She sounds brave."

Adam didn't respond to that, but instead got busy rinsing pans in the sink. There was a lot more he had to say on the subject, but he and Stacy weren't close enough to talk about regrets.

She imagined that Adam had a lifetime of them.

That went well.

Now she feels sorry for you. Great.

After feeding Stacy breakfast and cleaning up, Adam headed to the beach while she hit the shower. It was still early enough that he'd be able to catch Cole and Max during their surf time. He'd been asked to join in, but hadn't until today. Contrary to his former SEAL brothers, Adam didn't mind living in land-locked areas. He'd given up surfing a while back.

But he had a lot to share with the class today. He pulled into the parking lot and had only walked a few steps when he caught them both walking back, hauling their boards over their shoulders.

Yellow Submarine, Cole's yellow Labrador retriever, ran up to Adam. As usual, he acted as though they were long-lost friends, separated for decades.

"Hey, buddy." Adam bent to pet Sub, and watched as he rolled on his back and panted in joy at their reunion.

"Hey!" Cole called out.

"You're late." Max reached him. "And where's your board?"

"Shockingly enough, I didn't have one in Montana. I sold mine a while back."

"Time to get a new one." Cole clapped Adam on the back. "But we've both got a few spares if you—"

"I'm not here to surf."

Max and Cole exchanged a look. That "look" pissed off Adam. It was the look that said, "Which one of us is guarding his six today?" It was an "our brother needs help" look. *Leave no man behind.* They'd felt sorry for him for far too long. Now Stacy felt sorry for him, too, when he'd hoped that she could always remember him as he'd been with her that night. Carefree. Fun. Two words rarely, if ever, associated with Adam Cruz.

"It looks like I'm going to be a father."

"So, Stacy, the woman that showed up yesterday," Cole said. "That's your…? She's…?"

"Having my baby. Yeah." Adam shoved a hand through his short hair.

Ever since he'd had it cut, he felt a little naked. But while his long hair and beard worked in Montana, it didn't fly well in a kitchen.

Max, having already pretty much deduced the situation yesterday, simply loaded his board in the cab of Cole's truck. "How long have you known her?"

"Not long at all."

"So what's the situation? Your girlfriend?"

"I wouldn't say that. We're friends."

"Okay, well, that's good. Right?" Cole offered his hand. "Congratulations?"

"Sure, yeah. Thanks." Adam accepted the handshake, feeling odd. He hadn't had anything to celebrate in a long while.

"So what's the plan?" Max, the master planner, started with the easy question first. "Let us in on it."

"She's keeping the baby. That's the plan. And so… I suggested we get married." He stared past the men who were close as brothers and out into the vast gulf. "It seemed like the right thing to do."

"You suggested? And she said yes right away, huh? She signed right up for that," Max said, the sarcasm thick.

Cole palmed his face as if he couldn't believe Adam was truly *that* stupid. But hell, it had been a long time since Adam had done the romantic thing, and he was out of practice. Anyway, that's not what this was about. His marriage offer was logical. He didn't have much else to give Stacy, but he did have this.

"She's thinking about it. It makes sense. She's a self-employed writer without adequate health insurance and I've got great benefits with the VA."

"Adam," Max said. "You sound like you're talking about football scores or today's menu. How do you *feel* about this?"

"I'm having a kid." He held out his arms to the side. "Great. I feel great."

Max shook his head. "You're not ready for this."

"Apparently, I am. Or I will be. Either way, it's happening."

"You're going to be a father, yeah, I get it. That's great. But that doesn't mean you have to be a husband until you're ready to be one," Max said.

"That's where you're wrong. Are you telling me you wouldn't marry Ava if you got her pregnant?"

"But I *am* marrying Ava."

"Exactly."

"That's different. I'm in love with her." He crossed his arms. "Are you in love with Stacy?"

It wasn't fair to bring that up as a qualification or condition. These were special circumstances. Adam didn't think he could love anyone, not in his current condition.

"Look, I'm with Max on this. You shouldn't cheat yourself," Cole said. "Wait for the *real* thing to get married."

"You've both seen her. Do you really think I'm cheating myself?" Adam scoffed.

"If you're just doing this out of a sense of honor, then yeah. You deserve better," Max said.

"Look, I've asked her to give me a week to consider my suggestion. I'd appreciate it if you two geniuses helped me out. It's either that or looks like I'll have to move to Chicago."

"Chicago?" Cole dropped his board.

Adam might as well have said the moon judging by Cole's confounded expression.

"That's where she's from. She was headed that way until I talked her out of it."

"You just got here," Max said. "And you said you'd consider going into business with us."

"I said I'd think about it, yeah. But you know there's really only one way I'd be able to manage that."

"Mandy's life-insurance payout," Cole said. "I can't believe you've been barely keeping your head above water and won't touch what she left you."

Nobody understood, so Adam had stopped trying to explain. "This afternoon I'm calling to start the process."

He'd managed okay when he only had himself to

worry about. He wasn't picky about his living conditions and didn't date, so had no one to impress. But now he'd have a child and there was no way he would renege on that responsibility. He had no idea if he could even get Stacy to stay. That was the first order of business.

That's where these two bozos and their women might help.

"Can you get Valerie or Ava to take her shopping today? She needs clothes."

A few minutes later, with a sort of tacit truce between them, Adam followed the guys to the boardwalk in his truck.

The bucolic small coastal town of Charming was exactly as Max had described. Picture-postcard perfect with quaint lighthouses, bridges, jetties and piers jutting out to the sea along the wharf. Along the seawall-protected boardwalk, there were souvenir gift shops, restaurants, a small amusement park with a roller coaster and an old-fashioned Ferris wheel.

Max, somewhat of a grump at times, had assured Adam that Charming wasn't always *this* bright and shiny. But at Christmastime, well, Adam thought they were all one strand of Christmas lights away from a crashed electrical grid. It was obviously a great place for someone who enjoyed celebrating the holidays. Adam hoped it would be an attraction for Stacy, in addition to the mild weather.

He walked down the boardwalk with his friends toward the Salty Dog, Sub leading the way, barking out hellos to all of the vendors opening up their storefronts. When they arrived at the bar, Cole unlocked the steel gate and rolled it away.

The first photo Adam had ever seen of Charming was one of Max and Cole standing outside the Salty Dog on the night of their grand reopening. Max had texted him the image, telling him to drop by anytime and get a free drink on the house.

Until now, Adam never thought he'd be here, or see this place in person. Texas was a long way from Montana. A life away from the comfort and peace he'd found on the farm. But he'd been kidding himself for months because that illusion of safety hadn't been a part of his reality since the night he'd spent with Stacy.

And one of the reasons he'd left Montana was so that he might be able to forget her.

Chapter Six

After Adam left for work, Stacy took a drive through Charming. Yesterday, she'd been too exhausted to do anything but head to the Salty Dog, where she'd been told Adam worked. One thing about these small towns: everybody knew each other.

And the town itself, dare she say it, was *charming*. One main highway had the gulf on one side, and the town itself on the other. A lovely lighthouse in the distance appeared to be nonoperational. But two blue Adirondack chairs set outside had her imagining that some lucky person might actually live there.

It would be a cool place for her to rent and finish writing this albatross of a book. Maybe the villain could be pushed off the top of the lighthouse by the hero and wind up crushed on the rocks below. Or drowned. Yeah, drowned was better. Stacy shook her head.

No more plotting books while driving! Remember what happened last time.

Clearly, the boardwalk was the town's main attraction. Little cottage beach homes were scattered here and there, with banks and a few office buildings at one end of town. She passed a gallery named Artlandish, and Hot Threads, a yarn shop. Shoe Fly was quite obviously a shoe store and Get Nailed a salon and spa.

But she found nowhere to buy clothes. Which led her to a new and uncomfortable truth: she was going to have to find a place that sold *maternity* clothes. In order to avoid the pain of that latest truth, she parked near the bookstore, Once Upon a Book. Once upon a time, in fact, young Stacy had wished there were jobs for professional readers. But no one would pay her for that, so she'd wound up writing for a living.

It had been fun for a while, as she happily wrote one book after another. Then she'd had a hit.

After that, life got a whole lot more complicated.

She opened the door to the bookstore and the scents of paper, dust and ink invited her to come inside and stay awhile. Nowhere in the world smelled quite as cozy and warm as a bookstore.

"Hello there," said an older gentleman from behind the register. "Can I help you?"

"I'd just like to browse," Stacy said with a smile.

"Let me know if I can help. My name's Roy Finch."

"Thank you."

Stacy headed to the cooking and travel sections.

Once Mr. Finch was safely occupied, back to reading a tome entitled *The History of Texas*, Stacy inched her way over to the section that contained mysteries and thrillers. There, she found her most recent book. Three copies left, and she cracked one open. Her professional photo was in the back, with a pithy bio that made it sound like she breathed out books the way some people did carbon dioxide. Her photo was appropriately airbrushed to the nth degree, her hair perfectly cut and styled.

Safe to say no one would ever recognize her, not that she was a famous author, anyway. She used a pseudonym and no one but her fans and publisher knew of her. Stacy closed her eyes and stroked the cover of the book, hoping she'd transfer some of that amazing creative energy that had fueled her most successful book to date.

Unfortunately, she already knew it didn't work that way. It worked by putting her butt in a chair and her hands on a keyboard. *That's* how it worked. Instead, she was in a town she didn't know, trying to decide if she should get married to a *man* she didn't know. Dear Lord, her life was complicated. And to think she'd moved away from Chicago for fewer complications!

Two hours later Stacy had a stack of approximately ten books that she absolutely had to have or she would die. Most were fiction, but she'd tossed in a few on pregnancy. She'd shipped all of her books ahead to Chicago, and she wouldn't last a week with only what she had on her e-reader.

She set the stack on the counter in front of Mr. Finch. "I think that's it. I always make myself stop at ten."

"Goodness. Some people come in to take a nap because it's quiet in here. Nice to meet a fellow book lover."

"Yeah." Stacy snorted and pulled out her wallet. "Nice to meet you. I'm Stacy Hartsell."

Mr. Finch rang her up and the damage wasn't nearly as bad as she'd feared. He let her know that all the books were half off the cover price.

"We're struggling a bit keeping the doors open," Mr. Finch admitted, taking her card. "I volunteer my services. Since I'm retired it gives me something to do."

"That's kind of you."

"I love the written word," he said. "It's a passion. I'm actually something of a poet."

"Poetry is something I've never been able to master."

"You should come to our poetry readings. We've been meeting at a home here in town, but I'm trying to arrange a time here at the bookstore. I thought it might be a good way to bring in some business." He handed her back her credit card and the receipt. "We call ourselves the Almost Dead Poet Society."

"Now that's my kind of a group. Kind of morbid, isn't it?"

"We're all elderly senior citizens."

Stacy's smile froze. "I'm sorry. I thought the name was a joke."

They really were almost dead.

He gave her a wry smile. "It *is* supposed to be funny. But we do have young people join us from time to time. Keeps us young and fresh."

"I'll definitely drop in again soon and find out more."

If she wound up staying after the week. Back in her car, Stacy pulled out her phone and finally responded to all of Grace's many text messages and missed calls.

"So you finally decided to call me back! I was wondering if I should start calling area hospitals, but that was going to take me a while since I have a few *states* to cover. What if you were lying on the side of the road, all alone in the world, maybe even a Jane Doe if they couldn't find any identification on you?"

"Hey now, I'm the one who writes thrillers."

"Anything could happen!"

"And often does."

"Well, how did it go? Did you find him?"

"Yes, sure did. You're right, he's here. And he asked me to marry him."

"That's not funny. What happened?"

"I'm not joking." She waited a beat, listening to Grace's utter and complete silence. "He thinks it's a good idea. A marriage of convenience, how about that. Just like your books. He has health insurance through the VA, which, of course, would be better than what I have now."

More silence.

Stacy pulled the phone away from her ear, to check they were still connected. *"Hello?"*

"What did you *tell* him?"

"I said I'd think about it. He asked me to give him a week to consider it."

"You can't marry him! That's insane. No one should marry except for love."

Stacy sighed. *In a perfect world.* "Well, I'm not shocked to hear *you* say that. But some of us have to be a bit more practical."

"When I asked you to tell him, I didn't mean for you to rearrange your entire life for the man. He deserved to know, but you don't have to *marry* him."

"I know. It's just…starting to make sense to me."

"And then what?"

"We stay married until after our baby is born, then we divorce, and co-parent."

"Oh, so you're going to get married, have a baby and divorce within the space of a year, and you think that's a good idea?" Grace was shrieking a little bit.

"You don't much like this idea, do you?"

"It sounds like too many life-altering changes all at once, that's what I think. Having a child is going to be huge enough."

"I haven't decided what I'm doing. You'll be the first to know if I decide to get married. I promise."

"Why would you marry this guy? You spent one night with him and never wanted to see him again."

This was the tough part and Stacy didn't want to deal with any of this right now. "I never told you, but the thing is… I really liked him. I would have wanted to see him again."

"Then why didn't you?"

She closed her eyes. "I did a stupid thing. Made a lot of assumptions and didn't ask him the questions I should have."

"I thought it was a fling. A one-night stand."

"That's what it was supposed to be, but I would have liked to see him again."

Last night in bed, Stacy had let her mind wander and imagine what her life might have looked like had she never seen that framed wedding photo. Or maybe if she'd been a grown-up and asked him about the photo instead of jumping to conclusions. Maybe they would have worked it out. Maybe she and Adam would have started dating, and when she'd become pregnant, marriage would have seemed more of a likely solution.

"I—I don't know what to say."

"Say you'll have my back, because right now, I could use a friend."

Grace didn't hesitate. "You got it."

After hanging up, Stacy started up the car and pulled out. What she needed now was a little time to plot her book with her eyes closed. She'd just reached Adam's house when she saw two women walking toward the front door. One of them was Ava, the other a tall brunette. Both turned when they heard Stacy pull up and get out of the car.

Ava waved. "Hi! Remember me? This is Valerie, and we're here to take you clothes shopping!"

Oh, joy.

"Adam, your greatest fan said she just had the best burger ever. She said, and I quote, 'It must be the best turkey burger in the history of history. Please give Adam my compliments.'" Debbie picked up her orders and set them on the tray.

"How does she know *I* didn't cook it?" Brian asked.

"Oh, sugar, she assumes that when Adam is back here, he makes everything. He also hung the moon and makes the stars twinkle in the sky, don't ya know." Debbie winked and walked away.

"Must be nice," Brian muttered as he tossed French fries out of the basket.

Adam, and everyone else, knew Debbie was referring to Twyla. She was the daughter of the woman who owned Once Upon a Book and came in for lunch frequently. Adam had been about to ask her out on the very day that Stacy had shown up. For once, his timing was impeccable. His life was now far too complicated to get involved with anyone else, nor did he want to.

"Ask her out, Brian," Adam said. "I'm not interested."

"Why? Is it because of that babe I saw you with yesterday? The one with the long dark hair that reminds me of Megan Fox?"

Adam didn't like discussing his personal life but sooner or later everyone would hear about his situation. He just didn't know that the work kitchen was the right place to talk about failed birth-control devices and one-night stands with hot women.

Or the fact that he'd soon enough be a father for the first time. Gulp.

"Yeah. We dated when I lived in the Montana." That was the G-rated version.

"You lucky dog." Brian whistled.

An hour later they were nearing the end of the lunch rush when Adam heard Cole call out from the doorway of his back office next to the kitchen, "Hey, baby!"

Valerie must have arrived. She was a third-grade teacher and worked part-time as a waitress, so she dropped by often. Soon after, Ava's enthusiastic voice could be heard, as she gave one of her many announcements.

A business owner and president of the local chamber of commerce, she made a great cheerleader.

"Don't forget our toy drive for the children of Charming! I've put tags on our tree with some of their requests. Let's make sure we don't miss a single child, and that they all have a wonderful Christmas!"

Adam smiled at Ava's enthusiasm as he checked for his next order. She was a sweet woman with a good heart, and exactly what grumpy Max needed. Looking over the heat lamps into the thinning crowd, he caught Ava and Valerie sitting together at a booth.

Stacy was with them.

She laughed, tossing her hair back at something Debbie said as she took their orders. He *remembered* that laugh. The sound was wicked, throaty and sexy as hell. His heart rate kicked up with the memory, and his palms grew sweaty enough that he wiped them on his apron. Okay, this was ridiculous.

But the same night he'd met Stacy, he would have bet that he'd met her somewhere before. Sworn he already knew her. There was a certain synchronicity between them that he'd never experienced with a total stranger. With the number of countries he'd traveled to in his life, and the fact he never forgot a face, he'd thought it entirely possible they'd met before. But Stacy assured him over and over again that they'd never met. She would have remembered, she assured him.

He'd had to write off everything that happened that night to intense physical attraction. Magnetism. When she knew what he was about to say before he said it, that was the nature of two people who were drawn to each other like magnets. It had been so long that he'd simply forgotten how this sort of thing happened.

"Are you?" Brian asked. "Going to the tree lighting?"

Damn, Brian had been talking to Adam while he'd been spacing out about Stacy. Acting like a teenager with his first crush. What the hell was wrong with him?

"Um, sure. Yeah, maybe."

He vaguely remembered Max saying something about that, but last week Adam had planned to stay home.

"You should come. Ava makes a big deal out of it. She wants the staff to go, which means *Max* wants us all to go." Brian rolled his eyes. "Think of it as a company event. Building morale. Rah, rah."

"I'll think about it," Adam said, removing his apron. "I'm taking my break."

"Hey, how about that." Brian winked. "Didn't have to remind ya this time."

"I'm hungry," Adam lied as he washed his hands. But he wanted to check in with Stacy.

"I'll make you my very own burger, which if I do say so myself, is pretty day-um good."

"I know it is." Adam dried his hands and cracked a smile. "Thanks, bud."

He went through the swinging doors that led to the dining room. Cole was already waving to him from where he'd taken a seat on the bench beside Valerie. "Jingle Bells" piped through the speakers, one of the various holiday songs they had playing nonstop.

"Hey," he said, strolling up to the booth.

"Have a seat." Cole indicated the seat available next to Stacy.

Ava and Stacy were on one side, Cole and Valerie on the other. Max, Adam knew, was attending a meeting with their beer distributor in Houston.

"Thanks. I'm on my lunch break." He took a seat next to Stacy, who moved to give him room.

Either way, these bench seats were small enough that his leg was touching hers. She smelled delicious, like coconut, and a pull of longing hit him hard.

"We're just talking about the tree-lighting ceremony," Ava said. "You are coming, right?"

"Sure," he said, not wanting to be the town's grinch. "It's actually up to Stacy."

"I'm going, even though I told Ava I think the town is already dangerously close to a blackout."

Okay, that was eerie. He'd been thinking along the same lines not long ago.

"Then we'll both go."

"Oh, yay!" Ava clapped her hands.

"These kind ladies took me clothes shopping today," Stacy said. "On my own, I would have never been able to find the boutique."

"Glamtique is tucked away behind another building," Valerie said. "Not the best location."

"Lucy was excited to get the business," Ava said. "Most residents drive to Houston for the clothes shopping. Or order online."

A few minutes later, Debbie placed a burger in front of Adam. "There you go, Mr. Hottie."

"What was that about?" Ava asked.

"Don't know, but I think it's a bit of friendly razzing," Cole said. "Ever since Adam arrived, we've had a noticeable increase in patrons of the female persuasion. All hoping to get a glimpse of him."

Adam sent Cole a censuring look. He didn't want Stacy to think of him as a player, because despite their casual beginning, he never had been.

"That makes sense." Ava nodded. "Since Max is off the market."

"Hey, what am I? Chopped liver?" Cole said.

"You're the golden surfer boy, but Max and Adam have the sultry dark looks. All three of you are gorgeous," Ava said.

"And, baby, you've been off the market for years. You just didn't know it." Valerie palmed his chin.

Cole kissed her. Damn embarrassing the way those two carried on. Adam tensed beside Stacy and waited for those two to come up for air.

"Get a room," Adam said and took a bite of his burger.

They both laughed and broke the kiss.

"Hey, I'm the boss and business is good. I can kiss my fiancée wherever I like," Cole said.

"Before these guys took over the Salty Dog it nearly went out of business," Ava said. "I don't think it hurts when three former Navy SEAL team guys take over a struggling bar and grill."

"A SEAL?" Stacy turned to stare at him. "You said you were a soldier."

Chapter Seven

Stacy was gobsmacked.

Adam was a *sailor*, not a soldier, and he was special ops.

A Navy SEAL.

Her baby's *father*. Was her little girl going to be born with a crew cut, ready to kick ass and take names? Or what if her little girl was a little *boy*? Stacy swallowed. She was an author on *deadline*, and she needed an "easy" baby. Someone should have given Adam the 411.

"That's classic Adam," Cole said. "He probably also didn't tell you that he saved my ass more than once."

"Cole, cut it out."

His leg was pressed against hers, and Stacy felt him tense beside her.

"You saved my *life*," Cole said, not stopping, but then he held up both palms. "Okay, okay."

The mood at the table shifted from happy and merry, like a Christmas tune, to edgy and slightly moody. *The Nightmare Before Christmas* style. This was her wheelhouse and where she lived most days, but damn if she hadn't been enjoying all the lightness of the last few hours. It was refreshing.

Ava, for her part, seemed chagrined that she'd mentioned this at all. She bit her lower lip and fiddled with her place setting. Feeling bad for her, Stacy reached to squeeze her hand. Whatever had happened, whatever reason Adam had lied to Stacy, it had nothing to do with the sweet woman next to her.

"Well, I guess I should get going," Stacy said. "Thanks for the shopping therapy. It's been a full morning for me."

"You don't want something to eat?" Adam said.

Before he offered her *this* lunch, too, Stacy shook her head. "I'll grab something at your place. I'm not very hungry."

Adam stood and offered Stacy his hand to help her slide out. She didn't take his hand or look at him. There were so many things she didn't know about this man and every time she got a new revelation, a throb of guilt pulsed through her.

She should really know the father of her child a

lot better than she did, and hoped a week would be enough time.

Later, Stacy grabbed a few store-bought cookies from Adam's kitchen cupboard and drank a glass of milk. She hadn't been hungry at the bar, but two minutes into her drive, she'd been famished again. Having experienced "plotus interruptus" when Ava and Valerie showed up, she still had some writing to do. Or think about doing.

And there was still The Phone Call. Her mother had blown up her cell today with constant text messages. Stacy had texted back that she couldn't talk but would call her soon. Stacy hated confrontations and her mother tended to give her more than she could handle.

But she was alone now, with no Adam in close proximity to accidentally on purpose eavesdrop.

She picked up her phone and dialed. "Hi, Mom."

"Stacy! Finally! Listen, I just need an ETA."

"Um, well, it's going to take a little longer than I thought."

"How *much* longer?"

"It depends on how long it takes to fix my car," Stacy lied.

Please, baby girl, forgive me. You don't know what my mom is like when she gets going.

"Your *car*? Oh, no, what now?"

Stacy spun her story. She'd broken down on her way out of town, but the townspeople had saved her behind. Four strong men pushed her car off the road and then wanted to pay for her expenses to have it repaired. But, of course, she couldn't let them do that. On the other hand, how kind of these people. She'd happened upon some kind of rip in the space continuum in Charming. But Stacy pulled back a moment too late.

Right after she'd described in detail the Hansel and Gretel–like quality of the cottage she'd be staying in, rent free, her mother cleared her throat.

"Want to tell me what really happened?"

Stacy sighed. This is why she stuck to writing thrillers. "Adam wants me to give him a week."

"And who's Adam again?"

"Oh, my gosh, *Mom*. He's my baby's father. You know... I told you about him?"

"The sperm donor."

Stacy winced. "Don't *call* him that."

"Is this what you want? You want to delay Chicago for another week?"

"Well, I think I should know him a little better than I do. He's going to be the father of my child. I can't change that."

"Can't argue there."

"So it makes sense. Right?"

"But why a week?"

"I...he..."

This was the tricky part. Stacy realized that if she wasn't seriously considering the idea, she wouldn't have to tell her mother a darn thing. She'd just continue to allow Mom to believe this week was simply about getting to know the man who'd be her baby's father. Nothing more. Which meant, God help her, that she was seriously considering the idea.

"Adam suggested we get married."

Instead of the dead silence that had been Grace's response, her mother cackled with almost hysterical laughter.

"That's rich. Get married to a man you barely know just because you're pregnant? Good grief, honey, where did you *find* this guy?"

Incredibly, Stacy wanted to defend Adam. "That's not why he asked me. He's fully aware that we don't need to be married to co-parent. But he happens to be a good man, who wants to help. He has great insurance through the VA and if I'm his wife, that would be a huge help to me."

Mom's response was utter silence for a long beat. "That actually makes sense."

"Well, I'm not sure yet. I need some time to think."

"What's there to think about? It's a marriage of convenience. Get married, then come out to Chicago. You don't have to live with him. Just think of it this way—servicemen and their wives are sometimes separated for long periods of time. This could work."

Stacy hadn't even considered that option, which worried her. She was definitely off her game. The only thought running through her mind had been marrying Adam and staying here in Charming. But another option had presented itself and she wondered what Adam would think. Since he'd mentioned wanting to be an involved father, and following her to Chicago if need be, she'd guess that separating immediately after the marriage wouldn't be his first choice.

"Regardless. I need to give it some thought."

"Don't give it too much thought. Do you know any other men who'd be willing to marry you just so you could have their health insurance? Honey, I'd marry you if I could, for the insurance, but it doesn't work that way." She laughed at her lame joke.

"Gee, thanks, Mom."

Stacy had never been married, but she also hadn't actively pursued wedded bliss. She wouldn't have objected to marriage with Daniel. But since he'd been divorced just before they'd met, he'd been a little reluctant. Not wary of commitment, however, just the certificate *itself*, which he claimed ruined everything between two people who loved each other. He was a writer, too, and they'd seemed like the perfect couple for years. Book signings, publishing parties, trips to New York City.

Stacy thought she'd met her soul mate and sooner or later they'd get married. They were ideal for each other. She also thought it a wonderful thing that he was close with his ex-wife, Dominique. With no contentious divorce, no children or property to fight over, they'd called their divorce a "conscious uncoupling." Stacy had never heard of such a wonderful and smooth divorce. In fact, the three of them wound up being good friends. And it had been easy to like Dominique. A hair stylist formerly from Los Angeles, she gave Stacy discounts on both haircuts and products. If she was uncomfortable with the way Dominique sometimes discussed Daniel's sexual prowess, she told herself it was because she'd been raised in the Midwest.

After years of double dates and casual times, she'd walked in on Daniel and Dominique when they were in the middle of sex on *her* antique rustic breakfast table.

"I'm sorry!" Dominique had pulled back down her short skirt and run out of the house while Daniel zipped up.

"You *know* how much I love that kitchen table," Stacy said quietly.

Granted, it wasn't at all what she thought she'd say in that moment, which in the back of her webbed mind, she'd seen coming. After all, she lived in a world of plot twists. This wasn't even a good one.

"Stacy, I'm sorry. This is all my fault. I've never been able to resist Dominique."

"I'll have to burn the table now." She'd once imagined what she might feel like at a moment like that and had been shocked to find herself far less murderous than she'd assumed.

She simply felt distant, removed. And she wanted badly to leave but this was her house.

Daniel just kept talking. "There's just something about the sneaking around. Something about the illicit nature of forbidden sex."

"I wonder if I could find another one. You'll pay for it, of course." Stacy kept talking about the table as if that was the biggest issue.

Where they'd done the deed. Which was so damn insulting because she used to eat there. But because she hated emotional confrontations, and Daniel had forced her to walk right into one, she deflected.

"I feel terrible for doing this to you! You're a good friend to both of us and you didn't deserve this."

She pointed to the table, where she'd seen something she'd never be able to unsee. "I want this table out of here. Now. I'll eat on the floor."

"Would you stop talking about the damn table? I'm trying to discuss what just happened here!" He gripped her shoulders and shook her. "Don't you want to know how we got here?"

"No, I don't want to know how *you* got here. What I want is for you to get out and take the table with you!"

She'd never asked why he didn't want to have sex with *her* on their kitchen table. Apparently, as a couple, they weren't illicit enough. And there was always the chance that he still loved Dominique.

A month later, Daniel went back to Dominique, and they remarried shortly after, proving her suspicion. Mom, who'd naturally never liked Daniel, thought it was for the best. She'd wanted Stacy to move back into the town house she owned. But Stacy, who'd always been so close to her mother that Grace had later referred to their relationship as "codependent," wanted a new beginning.

She'd left Chicago and moved to Montana. From a safe distance, she could better deal with her mother. Keeping to herself, she didn't date anyone, or have any real friends until Grace.

And then she'd met Adam and understood the attraction of a clandestine affair. She understood a bit more how two people might be drawn to each other due to undeniable chemistry. One-night stands were not her thing, and never had been. She never slept with anyone until she knew them at least six months or longer. But every rule she'd ever followed was disposed of because she and Adam had an indescribable connection.

She'd been watching him come into the bar in Marion for months. Always alone. He never flirted with a woman, even if many flirted hard with him. Tall, like a linebacker. A little scary-looking with a full beard and hair as dark as espresso. It turned out that, far from frightening, he immediately put her at ease. His deep voice was warm and soothing.

He'd never talked to her before that night. He was a stranger she somehow felt she knew. He was familiar to her in ways she didn't understand, his warm body fitting perfectly with hers. It had all been a lie, apparently, or entirely one-sided. Given her history with Daniel, that framed photo was the last thing she'd wanted to see the next morning.

In her experience, she understood that separation and divorce, and maybe even death, didn't mean the end of love.

* * *

When Adam walked in the door after work, he found Stacy on the couch, her laptop open, hands on the keyboard. Eyes closed. She was snoozing. Her neck slumped to the side, a curly lock of dark hair covered one side of her face. He'd never had a chance to see her rumpled and sleepy look. Never had a chance at a morning after with her.

He leaned forward and brushed the hair off her face. She startled and woke suddenly, rubbing her nose, her eyes wide.

"Hey," he said, feeling a smile tug at his lips.

He was now getting what he'd missed. Sleepy. Dazed and a bit disheveled. Adorable.

"Adam."

His name rolled off her lips like a question. She might be trying to remember why she was irritated with him. He could do her the favor of reminding her, but thought best to segue right into the apology.

"I'm sorry that I didn't mention I was a Navy SEAL. It's just easier with civilians to say 'soldier.' I don't make those distinctions with strangers. But then later, when we were more, I didn't get a chance."

"Right. I can see that." She rubbed her eyes. "I wished you'd have told me before I had to hear it from your friends."

"You're right. We just haven't had much time to talk, but that's what this week is all about."

"It's just… I told you everything about me that

night. I'm a writer, out of a long-term relationship."
Stacy lowered her head and studied her hands.

"I wasn't keeping any secrets. But I'm just not a big talker."

"Well, you're going to have to start talking now."

"Right. And I will. Anything you want to know. I'm an open book."

"I don't know where to start." She closed her laptop and set it aside. "There's so much. I don't need a curriculum vitae from you. So you're a SEAL. I've done enough research in the past to know what that means."

"Okay."

"But…what about your wife?"

He should have known she would go straight there. "What do you want to know?"

"How long you were married, how you met, that kind of thing."

"Why? Mandy and I had a good relationship but that doesn't mean you and I can't also have one."

"I know." But she hardly sounded as though she believed that.

If she hadn't seen that photo, which must have seemed like a mini shrine to Mandy and his past, this wouldn't even be an issue. But it was an issue, and he could thank himself for that. No amount of self-flagellating was going to make the last words he'd said to Mandy forgivable, so he had to move on, as difficult as it was.

"We met when I was on leave and got married

about a year later. We were married for two years. Unfortunately, we were separated for much of the time due to work."

He was a *Reader's Digest* version kind of guy, so if she wanted more, she'd have to dig for it.

"And she's been gone for four years?"

"Yeah, almost." He ran a hand through his crew cut. Odd not to have a full head of hair and beard, especially with Stacy here. "Anything else?"

"Um, yes. Do you have any brothers or sisters? Parents?"

Hell. It was damn embarrassing how little she knew about him. He'd been a madman that night, going after what he'd wanted, hardly recognizing himself. He'd wanted inside of her like one of those sailors on leave people talked about. That hadn't been him. Ever. He'd always been a one-woman man, from his high-school sweetheart all the way to Mandy.

He'd never been casual with women. Never had a one-night stand before Stacy. Even that night hadn't felt casual for him. Until that morning, when he realized that Stacy thought of them as a hookup. Even now, he had the distinct feeling that Stacy didn't need him. It was a damn humiliating position to be in for someone who wanted to help. Who lived for helping.

"My parents are still married. Ernesto Cruz and my mother, Barbara. Everyone calls him Ernie. I have one sister, Bianca, who's married to Neal and has two children. I'm the youngest in our family.

Everyone but me still lives in El Paso." He paused. "You're an only child, right?"

She nodded. She'd told him everything that night, and it had all happened rather seamlessly. He could never manage that sort of thing.

"Like I told you, my parents divorced when I was young, and I grew up with my mother and grand-mother. We were the three musketeers." She sighed. "Okay, so I guess that's your family."

She did seem disappointed at the way he'd rattled it off. It would have been better in the natural flow of conversation, but they were trying to pack a lot into a few days. He wanted to get on with it. Later, if he was lucky enough for her to stay, he'd tell her more.

"And when did you sign up for the Navy?"

Quickly, he explained how he'd joined after high school. Met Max and Cole when they'd been re-cruited into special ops. The three of them, solid as brothers. They'd been through a lot, most of which he never discussed.

Like the fact that he had a medal or two, safely tucked away in his father's dresser drawer in El Paso.

Chapter Eight

A few days later, Adam still didn't have an answer to his suggestion of marriage. Once, he'd casually asked Stacy if she'd made up her mind, and she raised a hand in the universal stop sign and indicated that she would take every single one of the seven days to decide. By his calculations, she only had three days left, but he'd given her all the time she wanted. He understood that Stacy's mother would be waiting for her in Chicago, and she'd obviously have to give her a decision, too. The important thing was to get all the paperwork done so Stacy could book her appointment with a new doctor in January.

He'd filed for the life insurance, without telling Stacy, because he didn't want to imagine what she'd think about the fact that he'd only recently done so. Maybe she'd think he was completely disorganized. Either that, or she'd attached more significance to the situation. He simply hadn't filed because he didn't want to benefit from Mandy's death in any way.

After a quick dinner he cooked for them, Stacy went into the bedroom to change for the tree-lighting ceremony. She emerged wearing what she announced were some of her new clothes. And Adam swallowed. Hard. Should she look this *sexy* to him? Pregnant women didn't attract him in the slightest. He felt like an oddball freak.

Being the youngest, Adam didn't have a memory of his mother being pregnant. When his sister was pregnant, he hadn't been around. But some of his SEAL team brothers were already fathers, and they'd complain about how their wives' bodies had changed. From where he stood, Adam didn't see much of a change in Stacy. Her long legs were covered by dark jeans and she wore a loose top that couldn't conceal those amazing breasts. He tried to school his expression into one of disinterest, but had a feeling he'd failed when she gave him a smirk.

"Remember what I said. No fooling around."

"I remember," Adam said, opening the door for her.

How could he forget, when it seemed this was all she talked about? Okay, maybe it was all *he* thought about.

He'd been in Charming for a couple of weeks

now, just before Thanksgiving, so he'd begun to understand how the town loved its holidays. They'd started decorating the boardwalk on Thanksgiving Day. There were strands of white lights on every vendor's storefront, and an entire set of plastic reindeer, Santa and his sleigh suspended in the air across one side of the boardwalk. Signs everywhere proclaimed everyone should have a "Charming" Christmas. Ho, ho, ho.

As a kid, he'd loved Christmas. And his parents had put on a show, complete with his father dressing up as Santa for the neighborhood kids. His mother had participated in a huge production of the Nativity scene that included actual barn animals. The holidays were a big deal in the Cruz household.

He wanted that kind of wonder and amazement for his child. His *child*. Since the shock of the truth had worn off, Adam had been getting used to the idea. He still had a way to go, because there were a few phone calls to make and inform his family. However, he planned to wait out the week before he dropped the bomb. For his old-school Catholic parents, news of a pregnancy that went hand in hand with a marriage would go over a whole lot better.

Along the boardwalk, the waves rolled in and out on one side. On the other side were all the vendors. He tried to see the place from her eyes. Initially, he'd thought this excitement was over-the-top, but now he'd begun to have an appreciation for the sentiment. Sometimes holidays weren't celebrated enough.

"What do you think of all this?" He waved his hand in the direction of the kettle-corn store, now selling peppermint-flavored red and green popcorn. Every worker inside was dressed like an elf.

"It's homey."

"Special kind of place."

He tried not to sound as if he was selling Charming, but he did want to stay here. Cole and Max were right—he'd been a nomad for too long. Growing roots in a place like Charming would be good for him. *No more running from memories.* He would be a father and the idea terrified him as much as it excited him. Since he'd been stuck for the last few years, he couldn't exactly object to life pushing him forward.

"It's a little like Marion in some ways, without all the snow, freezing temperatures and mountains."

"Business doesn't slow down because of the weather, although hurricane season can hit hard here. Max bought plenty of insurance."

Up ahead, Adam spotted the huge tree in the center. Someone dressed like Santa walked around, handing candy canes out to kids. Fake snow dotted the bottom of the tree. That always made him laugh. Everyone thought snow was so romantic and scenic until the moment they had to shove several inches of snow off their vehicle, or the roof of their house caved in. Then snow lost all its magical appeal.

"If there's going to be a blackout, it will happen when they light that sucker." Adam pointed.

Stacy snort-laughed, which he found oddly attractive. They'd reached the gathering of folks around the tall pine, and a tall, but rather thin-looking Santa approached. Surely, they could have rounded up someone better than this.

"Glad you two made it," Max said from under his white fake beard.

Adam found it difficult not to laugh. "What's this? Santa Max?"

He lowered his beard and scowled. "Don't give me any crap. The Santa that Ava hired couldn't make it."

"We can't have a tree-lighting event without Santa, can we?" Adam tipped back on his heels.

"That's what Ava says." Max shook his head. "The things I do for love."

Max went off, handing candy canes out to the children, slowly making his way back to the grandstand. Valerie and Cole were wandering around arm in arm, attached to each other with some kind of super glue.

"Adam! Stacy!" Cole tugged Valerie with him.

"Hi, guys," Stacy said. "Thank you for inviting me. I feel a little like I've walked on to the set of a Hallmark movie. Are we the extras?"

"It's all Ava's doing," Valerie said. "I sometimes think she could have been a Hallmark card in another life."

"Welcome, everyone!" Ava boomed through a megaphone. "It's time for another annual Charming Christmas tradition. The lighting of the tree! So! Fun! This year our tree is donated by Oregon Tree

Growers of Grants Pass, and it's a beautiful Douglas fir. Before we hit the switch and light up the sky, you'll each get to place an ornament on the tree. Just reach in the baskets that the most handsome Santa *ever* is passing out. Find an ornament in there and put it on the tree. Tall guys? Help us out by reaching the higher branches. Thank you!"

Max handed out baskets and one eventually came to them. He and Stacy reached for the same ornament.

She laughed and let go. "You take it. I'll get another."

"No, it's yours."

He held it up by the red ribbon. The gold-plated ornament read, "Our First Christmas."

Adam stared at the second ornament he'd held in the last few days that reminded him of the first Christmas he'd spent as a married man. Everything inside of him locked up, froze, and panic seized him in short waves.

Guilt.

Anger, and so much pain.

Then he sensed something pulling on him and felt Stacy's hand on his arm. Warm. Squeezing. It shook him back to the present. He was here, in Charming, with a beautiful woman. His first real chance to move on, to move forward. And, God, how he wanted to.

"Adam?"

Her sweet face and narrowed eyes kicked him in the gut. She did not deserve this. "I'm okay."

"You can take another ornament," she said, her voice laced with tenderness. "Put that one back."

"No," he said, "I want this one. This is our first Christmas together."

He walked to the tree, where others were already placing their ornaments. Reaching up, he hung the ornament from a heavy branch. He motioned for Stacy to come close.

"Want me to hang yours, too?"

"Sure," she said, handing him an ornament in the shape of a deer.

He put it on a branch close to his ornament and, with some effort, turned to give her a smile.

It felt forced, but he hoped it counted, because he wanted this to be real.

Stacy had never seen so much pain etched on a man's face. A veil had crossed over Adam's eyes as he held the ornament, and then he was gone. Lost. In another place. Her heart ached and thudded hard, and she had to bring him back from whatever terrible place his mind had taken him.

She suddenly wanted him here and now, with her, and not wherever he'd gone in that ugly, dark moment.

He'd been enjoying himself, and had a dismayed reaction to all the wattage. He'd teased Max and smiled at Ava's enthusiasm on steroids. Strolling next to her, he'd seemed relaxed, the tension in his shoulders gone. She remembered the Adam she'd met the first time, the one that laughed at her jokes and understood her macabre sense of humor.

Maybe he's exactly who I thought he was.

But after the awkwardness of the ornament, she didn't know anymore. This man held on to a grief so deep she couldn't begin to comprehend it. She'd stepped into his life and created utter chaos when he needed peace.

"Santa, hit the switch!" Ava yelled, and the tree slowly lit from the bottom up, in a perfect symmetry of motion.

It was impossible to be the only one in the crowd who didn't ooh and aah at the sight.

"Beautiful," she said, taken back to the days as a child when she'd loved Christmas.

Almost without realizing it, she reached for Adam's hand. It was because no one should be lonely at Christmas, she told herself. She was here for him and whatever he'd been going through, because he was obviously going to be here for her and their baby. And he didn't have to be.

He smiled at her again, a little less stilted this time, and squeezed her hand.

"Thanks, everybody!" Ava was back behind the megaphone again. "Don't forget, next week, the sixtieth annual Christmas float-boat snowflake parade! Come see Santa in his very own float boat."

Float boat?

Stacy met Adam's eyes, quirking an eyebrow in question. But he was doing the same to her.

No idea, he mouthed.

"Is it just me or does that not seem much like a Texas theme? Snowflakes?" Stacy said.

"All I know is I would pay good money to see Max in a snowflake float boat. I can't miss it."

Max came up to them, fake beard lowered. "It's not going to be me. We've got the real Santa coming for that."

"Did you hear that, Mommy?" a little boy said. "The *real* Santa is coming!"

"Uh…" Max said as the kid and his mother hurriedly walked by.

The sound of hearty laughter from Adam was one of the most beautiful sounds Stacy had ever heard.

"Need help taking down that grandstand?" Adam pointed in the direction.

"Nah, Ava hired a crew." Max waved and went to join his fiancée.

"Do you want to walk around a little?" Adam said.

"Sure." The night was mild and cool, reminiscent of spring instead of winter. "You guys have gorgeous weather. It's strange not to need a parka in December."

"The fun never stops. I think that's the actual Charming boardwalk motto."

Many of the vendors were still open, their shops decorated to the hilt with snowflakes, trees and more lights. The amusement park rides on the other end of the boardwalk were still running. They walked along the seawall, the sound of seagulls cawing and foraging for food in the sand. The aromatic smells of fresh coffee, hot cocoa and popcorn competed for the number one spot.

"Look at this, Stacy." He stopped, then moved her in front of him. Hands on her shoulders, he pointed her to the smattering of stars against the clear black sky. "What a beautiful night."

They stood in silence for a few moments, listening to the sound of the roller coaster in the background. Families were out having fun, creating memories. She wondered what life would be like for her baby when he or she was old enough to enjoy amusement-park rides. What kind of a father would Adam be? Fun weekend Dad? Or the kind of wistful dad who spaced out every now and then when a painful memory pulled at him?

Either way, she had no doubt that he would love their child with all his heart. That much was in his eyes. And maybe this would be good for him. Heal him.

"How are we going to do this, Adam?"

He didn't have to ask what she meant. "However you decide."

"I've never been married before."

"I'd be honored to be your first."

Her first. Not her last. The thought of her first marriage as one of convenience was not at all what she'd pictured. Even for someone like Stacy, who was not particularly romantic, love had always figured into the equation. She thought she might be settling for what Adam could give her, but it was too late now. There was a baby to think about and she couldn't afford to be picky.

There were apparently other reasons to get married besides love. Like good health insurance.

"I can't help but feel like we've created a disruption for you. Maybe you'd planned to lead a quiet life here, and that's still what you want."

"I came here because a brother in arms needed my help. You're not disrupting anything."

"But if I want to move to Chicago, you'll follow me there, and leave all this behind. Your good friends. Their wives. That's not *fair* to you."

Lord knew Adam needed their emotional support and she had a baby to worry about. She'd help Adam all she could, but she couldn't be responsible for his mental health, too.

"Don't worry about that. I'll work it out. Max and Cole will understand. They're all about family."

"I didn't want to burst in on you and change everything. You know that, right?"

"This baby, *our* baby, changed everything. The baby changed your life and should do the same for mine. We both have a part. Like it or not, you and I will be tied together forever because of our child."

Forever. Stacy was beginning to like the idea very much, which scared her. She'd already been in love with a man who'd never let go of his first wife. Adam's wife was never coming back, but second place in a man's heart was not something Stacy would ever be willing to settle for.

Now, she was carrying Adam's baby, and the stakes were higher. She and Adam would have to get along one way or another. He was right. They were in this together out of circumstance. Maybe they could somehow make the best of it.

"You're right. The baby changed my life, and she'll change yours, too. That's how it should be."

"She?"

Stacy shrugged. "I've been thinking of her as a girl. It's just a feeling I have."

"A little girl would be awesome."

Once more, she recalled the lost look in Adam's dark eyes as he stared at the ornament, which had obviously triggered a memory. She wanted to help. She wanted to fix this for him. Stacy wanted to see that carefree guy that she'd met in Montana. A surge of tenderness tugged. *He* needed them—both her and their baby. She would somehow brighten Adam's life. That's exactly what she'd do. She wouldn't be too much trouble and only give him tiny glimpses of the happiness he'd obviously once had with someone else.

Because in a way, they needed each other.

Chapter Nine

Seven days after Stacy had breezed back into his life, Adam made a decision.

They were living like roommates, bumping into each other in the kitchen, eating meals together. He'd turned the spare bedroom into his own sleeping quarters because the couch was far too short for him. Eventually, he'd buy a cot. For now, he had a sleeping bag and a pillow, all he required for a good night's rest. Stacy didn't realize he'd been trained to sleep on a rock. She complained that he should at least have an air mattress on the floor, but understood there was no way in hell he wouldn't let her have the bed. She'd stopped trying to convince him that since she was shorter, she could sleep on the couch.

She often tried to draw him into conversation, and he found himself talking a little more every day. This seemed to be what she wanted from him and he would not fail Stacy. He might not feel worthy of her, but he would somehow have to convince her that he was.

This meant getting into the holiday spirit, like it or not.

After lunch, Adam grabbed his keys. "Will you be okay here for a while?"

"Of course." She sent him a censuring look that told him maybe he was overdoing it in the eager-new-father department. "Do what you have to do."

"Can I get you anything before I leave?"

"Adam, please! I have a lot of writing to do. I'm fine."

He held up his palms. "Okay, okay. I'm out."

Adam drove downtown in the Ford pickup that had made it all the way here from Montana. However, it would likely not live much longer, judging by a disconcerting rattle in the engine. Besides, he would need a safer family vehicle once the baby came. He made a mental note to look into that soon. But first, Christmas.

It was coming to his house.

A couple of weeks ago, Susannah had expressed dismay that Adam hadn't done any decorating.

"Ava *always* had the house decorated right after Thanksgiving." Susannah had shaken a finger at him as she stood outside between her outdoor light-up plastic Santa and tree.

"I'll get to it." Adam had waved her off.

He'd had no intention of getting to it, and assumed that this holiday would pass like all the others. But not this time. This time, he would do everything in his power to deliver Stacy a good Christmas. He was a man with a mission, and headed to the tree lot he passed every day on the way to work.

An old man wearing a Santa hat and a name tag that read "Johnny B." sat on an old milk carton near the entrance. "Howdy. We got Douglas firs, we got noble fir, we got some eight-footers and we got some Charlie Browns. Whatcha looking for, big guy?"

"Douglas fir," Adam said and walked past the old guy into the rows of trees.

He looked at a few and checked the tags, trying to find one with thick and full branches all the way around. It didn't take long to locate one that would do the job. He settled on a six-footer, then hauled it to the entrance.

Johnny stood and accepted his cash. "Need some help...nope, guess not."

"I could use some rope if you have it," Adam called back as he heaved the tree into the back of his truck.

"You new around here?" Johnny said, handing Adam some rope.

"I'm Adam Cruz." He removed his glove to offer his hand. "New cook over at the Salty Dog."

"Nice to meet ya. You rarely see a guy come in here by himself. Usually there's a gal picking out the tree."

"My girl—" Adam corrected himself. "She's pregnant, and I'm trying to surprise her."

"Congratulations, son! Way to go!" Johnny clapped Adam on the back.

A few minutes later, Adam realized he'd done his errands in the wrong order. He should have thought to buy strands of lights and ornaments first. Now, he'd have to stop at stores with a tree in his truck.

Adam loaded his shopping cart with ornaments, Santa hats, candy canes, tinsel, fake snow and even an outdoor decoration in the shape of a huge wrapped gift. He found everything he needed except for strands of lights. He went to three more stores, but every one he visited was out of lights. The residents of Charming had bought every single box! He wondered if he'd have to drive to Houston in order to do his civic duty and put up some Christmas lights.

"Hey, Adam!" Valerie was standing in line at the checkout of the third store, holding a box of lights in her hands.

"Hey" He pointed to the box. "Where can I get some of those?"

Valerie clutched the box to her chest. "I—I think it's the last one?"

"Yeah, it is. Sorry. Because of the Christmas float-boat parade, we sell out early every year," the clerk said, and shrugged.

"Guess I'll have to drive to Houston," Adam grumbled.

"Take these." Valerie held up the box of lights.

"I can't. You need them for your tree."

"No, actually, that's all done. I was just going to get Cole to hang some more lights around the outside of the lighthouse."

"More lights around the *light*house?"

Cole and Valerie lived in the town's only converted lighthouse.

"Well, outside so that…yeah, it was a silly idea." She laughed, shaking her head.

"I think Charming is having a love affair with Christmas lights."

"You can say that again." Valerie handed over the box. "Will one box be enough?"

"Yeah," Adam said with a smirk. "I'm sort of a light-strand minimalist."

"You have to decorate outside, too, you know," the clerk added, like the thought of not doing so struck fear in the heart of every resident of Charming. "It's all about the wattage."

"So that you can be seen from outer space?"

"Exactly."

As they walked outside, Valerie asked, "How are you and Stacy doing?"

"Great." Adam tossed the box inside the truck.

But not quite like he'd prefer. He was living with a roommate with whom he'd once had the most erotic night of his entire life. He supposed that night would have to last him forever now. She showed no inclination to do anything more than hold his hand.

"We're just a little worried about you. So many changes all at once. You moved, have a new job, and baby on the way."

"And Stacy and I are hopefully getting married."

"*Married?* I didn't know this. That's a lot of changes."

"The baby and the wedding are connected. I think you should count it as one big change."

Valerie nodded. "Okay. But did you know that huge lifestyle changes cause people a lot of stress? And the amount of big changes compounds the level of stress."

"Tell Cole not to worry about me. I'm happier than I've been in a long while. I have a mission and a plan."

"He just cares so much about you. You're one of the people from his past he's talked about the most. How he wished he could have helped you when…" Her voice drifted off, and it was clear she didn't want to finish that sentence.

He was trying to get past this—couldn't everyone *see* that?

"I'm moving on, Valerie. It's what everyone who cares about me has been waiting for me to do, and now that I've done it, nobody can accept it. I'm having a baby, hopefully getting married, and that's all there is to it."

"But… I know you're thinking, what's the big

deal? These are all good changes, and they are. It's just that every change, good or bad, throws the body into turmoil. There's actually a chart that measures stress levels by life events. A high score means a higher risk of illness in the future."

"You're a *third-grade* teacher?" He scratched the bristles on his chin.

"Psychology is a hobby of mine."

"Thanks for caring." He tapped Valerie's shoulder. "I'm really okay."

He might have to sit down and have a long talk with Cole and Max. He'd need to explain that just because he'd chosen to be out of touch for the last few years, that didn't mean he couldn't cope with life. Somehow, he'd been gifted with another chance.

And he would not fail this time.

Stacy rubbed her hands together and prepared to hit Send on the email to her editor. The proposal was complete, including her revisions. She dared to hope that this was the start of another bestseller. The first few chapters were filled with tension, mystery and darkness. She was back in her wheelhouse.

"Okay, that's it. No matter how much harder I try, I don't think I can make this any better. I've written the best proposal I can at this time in my career."

Her finger was poised about the touch pad, then she clicked Send. This would trigger the second payment on her advance, money she needed yesterday. She'd been operating out of her dwindling savings account for weeks. She was supposed to be in Chicago by now, where her mother would take care of the household expenses. Adam probably wouldn't take money from her, of course, but she'd force him to accept some. It wasn't his job to take care of her the way he had been. He'd bought all the groceries, put gasoline in her tank and brought her takeout after every shift. Not to mention the rent and utilities.

Every time he saw her, he asked how she was feeling and if he could get her anything. Rather than appreciating his doting on her, this only annoyed her. Which meant something else was burrowing under her skin, the real problem, and she thought she understood what.

Her deadline had arrived. Of course, she could take more time if she wanted to, and Adam wouldn't mind. But she did. He was right in that they had a clock running, because there would be paperwork to turn in for her health-care coverage. And she was due for an exam next month. Her mother, of course, had called and texted daily, asking whether Stacy had made her decision. The kind of relationship she'd always had with her mother had her expecting that Stacy would confide in her more than she had lately. Instead, Stacy had stubbornly chosen to take every single one of the seven days of the week to make her decision.

Everything in her screamed that logic should drive her decision, and that logic said marrying a military man was a no-brainer. But it wasn't quite that simple for her. If anything, this week had proved that her feelings for Adam ran deep. When she caught him studying her with those deep brown eyes, everything inside her screamed *no!* She didn't need him to look at her in a sultry way that made her want…things. That made her want *him*.

His heart is not available to me, or anyone else. Don't take it personally.

But every other part of him…um, yeah. She wouldn't mind some of that. One more night like the first one they'd had together. When they'd both been carefree, and wild, and so into each other it felt a bit like magic. Now, of course, life was different. Far from carefree, it was complicated in a way she'd never experienced before.

But a wedding and a baby usually went along with couples who were already in love, who couldn't wait to get home and tear off each other's clothes. She figured that on the night of their wedding, Adam would say goodnight to her at the doorway of the bedroom, as he'd done every night. All for the best. She understood. It didn't mean she had to like it. Her crabbiness lately hadn't been just due to pregnancy hormones—living with a hot guy that she had to keep her hands off had also been a factor.

He was adorably sexy in the morning, walking like a zombie before he'd had his coffee. He always offered a slow, sleepy smile through hooded eyes. Beard bristle dusted his chin and jawline. He had such thick facial hair that by the end of the same day he had sexy stubble. She'd only lived with him a short time, and she already nearly had to sit on her hands to avoid touching him. He'd held her hand, and took every opportunity to touch her casually, even if they were just passing each other in the hallway. He'd lightly put his hand on her back for a few precious seconds. Pure torture for Stacy.

She was jolted from her fantasies when the door shot open and Adam rushed in, hauling a Christmas tree behind him. He stood it up inside the doorframe. Nearly his height, it was the bushiest thing she'd ever seen. A perfect shape—full at the bottom, narrowing toward the top.

"What the—"

"Got us a tree!"

"I can see that," Stacy said, a bit incredulous with his sudden rush of holiday spirit.

Pine needles scattered on the hardwood floor as he moved it toward the window. The fresh scent of pine took over the small house.

"This looks like a good place, right?"

"Sure. Um, that's a lovely tree."

"Yeah. I thought so, too." He then propped it against the wall and headed back to the front door. "I've got a few more things."

She followed him outside, where a few more things turned out to be a large box and several bags.

Susannah emerged from next door and crossed their shared lawn. "Now that's more like it, young man! Better late than never. The spirit of Christmas has descended on you."

"Yes, it has, ma'am. Yes, it has."

"Do you need some help carrying all this inside?" Stacy asked as she waved to Susannah, whom she'd seen only in passing.

"From you? No, go inside and kick up your feet. Relax."

"I *have* been relaxing," she said through a stiff jaw. "Let me *help*."

He seemed surprised that she didn't want to sit on her butt forever, but handed her a light plastic bag... filled with candy canes. She resisted rolling her eyes.

"Hey, Mrs. Ferguson, have you met Stacy yet?"

Stacy tried a smile. "Nice to meet you."

"Call me Susannah," she called out. "Lovely to meet you."

"We're having a baby," Adam announced, as if talking about the weather.

"I guess...congratulations?" Susannah said.

"Thanks!" Adam carried the big box in the house and Stacy turned to follow him.

"Oh, Stacy?" Susannah said. "Mr. Finch says you're a dedicated reader. You might want to come to the next meeting of our senior-citizen poetry group. We always love an audience and young people are the best. You probably know Valerie? She always attends to support her grandmother."

"I'd love to come to the next meeting."

For crying out loud, what else did she have to

do? She'd completed her proposal and had to wait for editor notes. She could either sit home and watch Adam knock himself out trying to wait on her, or attend a poetry meeting, eat cookies and drink punch. Besides, she'd always been fond of the older generation. She still missed her grandmother fiercely even though she'd been gone for ten years.

Susannah cocked her head. "You look so familiar."

Stacy's spine stiffened. Maybe Susannah had read her book. Though she looked nothing like the photo in the back, and used a pen name, at some point it was possible that someone *would* recognize her. Especially since Adam knew exactly who she was and what she did for a living.

"Guess I have that kind of face."

But sooner or later she'd have to let Adam's family and friends know that she wrote books in which she often killed off characters with violent deaths.

She wasn't looking forward to that.

Chapter Ten

"Are those *all* the lights?" Stacy studied the tree as Adam straightened it in the stand. They would barely be enough lights for this bushy tree.

"Let's not talk about it. I was lucky to get these."

"All sold out, huh? Are you really surprised after the other night?" She picked up the box and turned it over in her hands.

"Not at all. I'm a little late on all this." He came around from behind the tree and took the box from her, then tore it open. "Have you ever heard the expression 'less is more?'"

"I have, sure, but I don't think the town of Charming has."

Adam plugged the lights in, then began throwing the strand around the tree, willy-nilly, and with absolutely no finesse. It was a little like watching a mountain man primp.

"Um, need some help there?"

"No, I've got this." He tossed a light, then pushed it into the branches. "In my house, this was my dad's job. Then my mother and the rest of us put up the ornaments."

"Well, in my house it was the woman's job to do it all. I can do this, and it's annoying me what little care you're using to put up these lights."

He peeked around from behind the tree. "Huh?"

"We have to *conserve* because we only have this one long strand." She went hands on hips.

"I thought that's what I was doing."

"Oh, my gosh. Let me show you how it's done." She rolled up her sleeves, tucked her hair behind her ears and prepared to make a sappy mess out of herself.

She removed what he'd done so far and started over. Each strand was placed delicately on a bough and then circled with care around the tree. Adam helped by following her, holding the long strand.

"At this rate we'll be here until midnight," he muttered.

"What else do you have to do? Go ahead and do it. It's worth taking your time to do the job right."

"I think that's exactly what you said to me the first night we spent together."

She froze and every muscle in her body squeezed

with the memory. "Thank you for reminding me. You do take your time on certain occasions."

"When it matters." His deep voice was velvet smooth and set off all manner of alarms in her.

She could almost hear him whispering in her ear... *Do you like that?*

"I've never seen you blush," Adam said from behind her.

"I'm not *blushing*."

He snorted. "Okay."

She bumped into him since he followed so closely. There was his hand again, low on her back as if to steady her. Good thing her hands were occupied, or she might be tempted to touch him, too.

She desperately needed a change of subject. "By the way, I don't want everyone to know what I do for a living yet."

"Why not?"

"I'm going to be the mother of your child. Do you really want everyone to know that I write books in which I kill people off violently?"

"Why not? It's *fiction*."

"Poor man. You're so naive. Some people make judgments."

"Surely they don't believe *you're* a serial killer. That would be a stupid thing to do. Kill people, then write books about it."

She had to laugh. "No, but it's more like they wonder what kind of mind I have to think up some of the scenarios I do."

"That's true. I read your book and I wondered where you came up with that bathroom scene. Pretty gory."

She stopped moving and Adam bumped into her again. "You read my *book*?"

"Sure did. After you gave me the kiss-off, I was curious about you. And all I had was your book."

"You weren't given *permission* to read my book. I didn't want you to read it."

"Why not? It was good 'edge of your seat' stuff. But gotta admit, had I read it first…not sure I would have gone home with you that night." He shook his head, a smile tugging at his lips. "Okay, I'm lying. Still would have taken you home."

"I can't *believe* you read my book. Now you think that I have a dark mind."

"Actually, I love the way your mind works. You make me laugh as much as you scare me."

He was still having fun with her. But since he could likely kill her with one press of a finger to her larynx, naturally he wouldn't be afraid of her sick mind.

"My books are personal. Private. That's why I use a pen name."

"Stacy, I've been inside you. I know what you sound like when you orgasm. We're having a baby. I don't think it gets much more personal than that."

She cleared her throat because damn it all, he was right. "Arthur Miller once said that the best writing an author can do is when you embarrass yourself.

So I'm constantly trying to do that. And I don't need you *reading* about it."

"Fine." He held up his palms. "I won't read any more of your books."

"And don't tell your mother! Or your father. Or anyone else you know."

"It's surprising you've sold any books at all." He shook his head slowly.

The lights up, they both stood back to examine the tree. They were white lights, and as they twinkled and blinked, they softly lit up the tree.

"Perfect," Adam said. "You're the tree whisperer."

"This comes from not having a man around for most of my life. I also know how to change my oil, fix a leaky faucet, carve a turkey and kill a spider."

"Guess I'm lucky to have good swimmers," he said, voice heavy on the sarcasm.

"Of course, I want a man. I just don't *need* a man. Shouldn't it be that way?"

He didn't answer, but simply bent to pick up a box of ornaments, which he handed to her. They were glittery red balls. Grateful for casual ornaments that didn't have any particular heart-wrenching meaning attached to them, she carefully placed one on each branch, separating them so they wouldn't all crowd together. There was an art to ornament placement.

Adam placed the star topper on the tree with ease, then got busy placing candy canes around the tree in no order whatsoever. They worked quietly in a sense of peaceful rhythm and she only occasionally chided him for placing a candy cane too close to an ornament.

"What were you like as a kid?" she said. "Did you love Christmas?"

"Of course. I was the kid who fell asleep on the couch by the fireplace waiting for Santa Claus to show up."

"Aw, that's adorable."

"Well, I was six." He bumped into her hand as he attempted to put a candy cane on the same branch.

She met his warm eyes and grinned. "I was here first."

"Go ahead, your highness. And what were you like as a kid? What can I expect from the little girl you think we're having?"

"Hmm. Just think of a dark-haired, shorter Ava and I think you've got little Stacy."

His neck swiveled back. "What the hell happened?"

"Okay, wise guy. My grandmother made the holiday special. She baked cookies and wrapped anything that wasn't moving in Christmas wrapping paper. Even the prints on the wall. All very festive."

"You were very close to your grandmother."

It wasn't so much a question as it was a statement.

"She helped raise me. For so long, Nana, my mom and I were the three musketeers. I was devastated when she died. It felt like I'd lost my rock. My compass." She said this for Adam's benefit, so he'd see that she understood grief, and wouldn't mind lending an ear.

"I'm sorry."

"So I know what it's like to lose someone."

"I think we all do." Adam stared a little too long at a branch.

Her heart hurt, and she pictured little Adam. Falling asleep waiting for a fantasy. Like most children, he'd had hope and a belief in magic. A younger Adam hadn't yet experienced the world as the often unhappy and tragic place it could be. He hadn't experienced the grief and loss of losing someone he loved.

"Adam, why are we doing this?" She bumped his hand to get his attention.

Predictably, he snapped out of it. "What do you mean?"

"You're trying too hard. Running out to get a tree and all these decorations. It feels like you're running away from something."

"Wrong. I'm running *toward* something." He met her eyes.

She wasn't sure she could believe that. "You don't need to keep things from me. I'm not too precious or tender to hear how much you miss her."

For the first time, she saw a flash of anger cross his gaze. Ah, yes!

We're getting to your layers now, Adam.
Show me who you are.

"Stacy," he said patiently, moving toward her. "Let

me tell you something. I'm here with you right now, and that's exactly where I want to be."

"Thank you, but—"

"No *buts*." He tipped her chin and forced her to look at him. "I lost someone, which is something that happens to nonmilitary spouses often. It just so happened to me in reverse. But it was a while ago, and I'd like to move on with my life if you don't mind."

Translation: stop talking about this, Stacy.

"Fine, Adam. That's fine." She took a deep breath. "Today is one week since you suggested we get married."

"I realize that." His hand dropped to the back of her neck and he simply studied her. "And?"

"And I've thought about this a lot."

After the baby was born, Stacy would move to Chicago. By then, maybe Adam would be in a better place.

"So have I."

"Okay," Stacy said. "I'll marry you."

He blinked, then gave her a big grin.

And as it turned out, Adam Cruz had a heart-stopping smile.

Later, after Stacy had gone to bed with the tree entirely decorated the way she wanted, Adam took a seat in the darkness and studied the tree. And then, while alone, he allowed the memories to assault him. Mandy, telling him she'd signed up for Doctors Without Borders because she was so proud of him and wanted to do her part in the war effort.

His absolute shock when he'd learned how close they'd be to the action.

Unacceptably close.

"Don't go. You do not want to be here. Hell, I don't want to be here," he'd told her on one of their scheduled talks.

"I know you're worried, but Dr. Mandel has taken his team there many times. We'll be fine."

Of course, they had *not* been fine at all.

It should have been him, and not Mandy or the other doctors, and all the other health professionals who only wanted to help. Adam was there for his own reasons, and none involved his great love for all of humanity. He loved and protected his *friends*. His brothers. He had nearly tunnel vision when it came to that, until one incident snapped his eyes open.

While Adam was busy helping everyone else on his team, keeping them safe, guarding their sixes, he'd failed to protect the one person he should have never failed. She should have been his primary responsibility and he'd failed spectacularly. He'd had only one Christmas with Mandy, since he'd been deployed on all the others. Theirs had been a short marriage.

Now, the potential to have Stacy and their child in his life stood before him like a lifeline and he desperately wanted that. He wanted to be worthy of her. Of them.

Maybe Stacy was right, and he'd been trying too hard. But damn, he felt like a drowning man who'd been thrown a life preserver. Stacy was his link to a life and everything that meant heart and soul. But it wasn't fair to hold her responsible for his happiness, or their baby.

"Fake it 'til you make it" might be acceptable on some levels, but it wouldn't be enough for Stacy. She was too smart, too witty, too engaged with life to fall for any substitutes. She saw right through him and the knowledge that he still held on to the past. He had to get over the regret, which was tougher to do because of the guilt that wouldn't let him go. And he wondered how he could ever forgive himself.

Not just because he'd failed to protect Mandy, but because of the ugly words he'd said at the end of their last conversation.

"You're ridiculous," he'd finally said to her, lashing out in anger and frustration. "Do you think all your medical knowledge is going to save you here? No one walks into this mess willingly. It never fails, whether it's a news crew I have to escort, or a doctor who means well, you all get in the way. Let me tell you something, Mandy, we don't want you here. *I* don't want you here!"

As it turned out, they were the last words he'd ever say to her.

Face it, he'd never been known for his timing outside of a battlefield. Not then, and not now.

Time to go to bed and hope the nightmares

wouldn't chase him. He peeked in on Stacy, who'd uncharacteristically left the door ajar. She was fast asleep, one leg thrown over a pillow. A wave of longing hit him fast and sharp. *He* should be that pillow. But she was here now, and staying. Marrying him. And that was good enough for now.

So he would get married again. This time he wouldn't fail as a husband. He'd protect Stacy and their child. He'd make himself indispensable to both her and his baby, so that if she chose to walk away, at least it wouldn't be easy.

"Don't get upset, but Ava and Valerie are throwing you two a reception," Cole said to Adam a week later. "I know you didn't want this to be a big deal, but I'm also sure you're not too surprised."

They were both sitting at the bar after closing time, having a drink together. Sub, who often spent Cole's shifts in the back office, was lying like a lump at Adam's feet.

"I would expect nothing else." Adam took a pull of his beer. "Let's just keep it small."

"At our house."

Adam had been inside the converted lighthouse and it was impressive, with a repurposed former ship's staircase, portholes for windows and the old-fashioned viewing telescope on the second-floor deck. It was the perfect house for a former Navy SEAL. Stacy would like it, too, making it easy to agree. At the same time, he worried this wedding was reeling out of control. It was supposed to be quick and simple. A marriage so Stacy could have his health insurance. Not just health insurance for their baby, but both mother and child. The way it should be.

Stacy wanted simple, quick, and he'd agreed. All he wanted was to be married to the mother of his baby. But the next thing he knew, his parents were coming down for the wedding. They were over the moon when they'd learned Stacy was pregnant, just as he'd suspected they would be. Then his sister decided she and her family would come along, too, since the children were out of school for winter break, and they hadn't been down to the coast in a few years. Next, Stacy's mother insisted they wait for her to attend.

Ava was working double time on pushing all the pesky government paperwork through with the help of the mayor. The day after she agreed to marry him, they'd filed for their marriage license, which had a 72-hour waiting period. Turned out that Charming had a rather quaint city hall downtown, so beautiful that many larger weddings were held there. But even with Ava working her best at finding them an opening with an available justice of the peace, their guests still had to make airline reservations, and book hotels.

"My friend Grace is also coming from Montana," Stacy had said to him this morning.

"Okay, so how many does that make now?"

"Two thousand?" Stacy sighed.

Adam ignored the sarcasm and buttered a piece of toast for Stacy. "By my count we have sixteen."

"I didn't want this wedding to turn into something this complicated," Stacy said.

"Neither did I, but we'll work it out. It will be fine."

"I'd like to believe you, but when Ava is involved, I worry nothing can be low-key," she'd said.

Now, Adam rolled his shoulders and continued discussing plans with Cole. "Might as well have a small party, though it's getting awfully close to Christmas."

There was only one date Ava had been able to snag from a local judge, who was doing the mayor a big favor. Adam's family would arrive the day before the wedding, Stacy's mother and friend on the day of the wedding.

"How are you handling all this? If it were me, I'd be nervous. I'm getting married, but I've known Valerie for what feels like forever."

Adam remembered being nervous once before because he actually hadn't known Mandy for long, either. She was a doctor, and he was a Navy man. There were plenty of people who didn't believe them to be a good match and he'd had his own last-minute doubts.

"This isn't the first time for me."

"True enough. And you've always been ready for marriage, haven't you? The rest of us were having a good old time dating and you were always out there looking for Mrs. Cruz."

"I dated plenty. Enough to know what I wanted."

"Just hate to see you rushing into this. What's the big rush?"

"Stacy is due for another doctor visit next month and I don't want her paying out of pocket like she has been. It's my turn to step up and take care of the mother of my baby."

"And after the baby's born. What's the plan?"

"Stacy will want a divorce. Then we can co-parent."

He was trying not to focus on being a weekend dad. And if she moved to Chicago as planned…he'd have to follow. How else could he be a part of his child's life? He wouldn't be content with summers.

Cole slapped a shot glass on the bar. "That's what I'm worried about."

"I'll be okay."

"You've had a lot of loss in your life and I hate this for you. You're already planning a divorce and you're not even married yet."

"Hate it all you want, it's happening."

Cole sighed and poured himself a shot of whiskey. "Max and I wanted you to buy in to the business but that was before all *this* happened."

"It's actually what's made me realize that I have to do something with the rest of my life."

After Adam's last Navy contract, he'd actually been offered a position involving a high level of security clearance in Washington, DC, but had turned it down. A series of odd jobs had followed. As a short-order cook, gardener and ranch hand, to name a few. Anything that kept him away from all the security enforcement positions that kept being offered. He was done with all of it.

"With your résumé and experience, you could do anything you want, and you know it." Cole raised his glass in salute.

"Once the insurance check arrives, I'll buy in."

"You sure?"

"Absolutely. It's time for me to find another mission. This will be the best chance for me to provide. I *want* to be a good father and I think I will be."

"No doubt about that." Cole pinched the bridge of his nose and briefly closed his eyes. "I wish you wouldn't pull this guilt trip on yourself. None of what happened to Mandy was your fault."

"Maybe not, but the way I talked to her? *That* was my fault. It was the last memory she had of her husband, telling her off."

"You were angry and worried."

"That's no excuse. I won't make that mistake again."

"That's the problem, bro. You're going to make some mistakes and that's got to be okay with you."

"Sure."

"But I have to admit, it's good to see you this animated again. Happy. She's obviously a special woman. How did you meet her?"

For the first time, Cole heard the whole story. Adam didn't hold back much, other than the highly personal. Not the intimate details about Stacy being a wild woman in bed, satisfying him like he'd never been before. He'd never been raunchy when talking about women.

Cole gaped through the story but then let out a loud laugh. "Incredible. Just your luck. You waited this long to sow your wild oats and then you get the woman pregnant."

"I don't think she'd like people to know how we met, so this is between you and me. Oh, yeah, and she's an author, but I'm not supposed to tell you that. *Also* between you and me."

"An author? Why wouldn't she want anyone to know that?"

"She's sensitive about what she writes." Adam shrugged. "They're thrillers. I read one and let's just say she's pretty damn good. Had *me* checking closets for a couple of days."

"Full reconnaissance?"

"Just about." This time, it was Adam who laughed.

Chapter Eleven

The night before the wedding was the Charming float-boat Snowflake Christmas parade. Adam's family had already arrived, renting rooms at the Lookout, the only hotel in Charming. To say his mother was anxious to meet Stacy would be an understatement. Adam had tried to calm her down, but without much success. Adam's father, for his part, seemed to view this as just another family event.

On the drive to the boardwalk, Stacy expressed her nerves with constant movements: flipping the visor down to check her lipstick in the mirror, fiddling with her hair, literally wringing her hands.

"What if your family doesn't like me?"

"They're *going* to like you."

"I worry they'll compare me to your first wife."

At that moment, he reached for her hand across the console. Both to keep at least one of them still and to reassure her. "There's no comparison. You're a completely different person than she was."

"That's what I'm afraid of!"

"In a good way. You're different in a *good* way."

She bit her lower lip and threw him a glance filled with doubt. "I am different in one spectacular way. I'm *pregnant*."

"True, that does give you an edge with them."

"An *edge*? I got knocked up before we were married. How do your old-school parents feel about that?" She let go of his hand and gripped his forearm tight enough for him to wince. "Oh, my God, Adam, your parents can *never* know how we met."

"We're in agreement there." That night had been out of character for him.

"I hope you told them that we met in the small town of Marion, where everybody knows your name. Like *Cheers,* but with mountains."

He'd already done that, along with a white lie that they'd dated for a few months before getting serious. "Are you still firm that we can't tell them you're an author?"

"Well, I can't lie to your family."

"Thank you."

"*If* they ask, I'll tell them. Let me be the one to do it."

Later, after the flurry of introductions, Adam's

mother wanted two things: to hug Stacy, and to ask for permission to touch her stomach. Stacy kindly agreed, and at that point Adam realized *he* hadn't even touched her belly. Or even asked to, which he should remedy at some point. Even though she liked to keep her physical distance, surely, she'd grant him this one request. Probably.

"I can't believe it," his mother said, clasping both hands together, as if praying. "Adam's child. I've waited so *long* for this moment."

Dad reached for his trusty handkerchief, something he never left home without, and handed it to his wife. *"Querida."*

Mom dabbed at her eyes. All four of them were sitting in a booth at the Salty Dog before the boat parade began. Valerie was working a shift tonight, and Adam watched the little dynamo waitress flit around the room, laughing and chatting with everyone.

"So what do you do, Stacy?" Adam's mother said.

"I'm a writer."

His mother exchanged a quick look with his dad. "A writer! How glamorous."

"Oh, no. Not so much." Stacy fiddled with her place setting. "I'm not famous or anything."

"Not yet." Adam's mother patted her hand. "Maybe you could write a book about pregnancy. So many books are written by male doctors who don't even have children. They certainly haven't given birth and have no idea what they're talking about. I'll bet yours would be a bestseller."

Great. Mom thought Stacy wrote nonfiction. She probably wouldn't discourage this.

"That's a good idea. I should be taking notes." Stacy held up her fingers. "Morning sickness, check. Weight gain, check. Movement, check."

Adam was just getting over the realization that she'd been sick during this pregnancy when he zeroed in on the movement part. He really should start asking more questions if he wanted to be along for more than the ride.

"It's just about the right time to feel the baby move," his mother said. "Some first-time mothers can't tell, so good for you."

His baby was moving. Moving.

"Hiya, folks," Valerie said with the cheery attitude and smile that made her one of the best waitresses he'd ever worked with. "I'm Valerie. Y'all ready to order?"

"Folks, this is Valerie Villanueva. She's Cole's fiancée."

"Oh, Cole's fiancée!" Naturally, Mom had to climb out of the booth to hug Valerie. "I *love* Cole."

If there was a person alive that his mother wouldn't bear-hug, Adam hadn't met them yet. Valerie smiled and chatted for a few minutes and took their orders, and the conversation soon turned to the wedding day.

"I want to know what I can do to help," Mom said.

"It's just a small wedding," both he and Stacy said at once.

"Look at you two, already finishing each other's sentences." She practically levitated with joy. "I'm glad that you're putting the emphasis where it belongs. It's not the wedding that matters. It's the *marriage*."

"Right," Stacy said, not so accidentally bumping his foot. "The marriage."

Adam went still. Stacy was going to kill him. But his mother had assumed this was a love match and ran with it. He didn't want to discourage that, either. All details were on a need-to-know basis. Mom didn't need to know. The whole convenience thing wouldn't sit well with her.

"Too many brides need the perfect dress, the perfect veil." She tapped her husband's chest. "Oh, Ernie, what's that show that Bianca watches all the time?"

"*Say Yes to the Dress*?" Stacy said.

"It's the one about godzilla."

"*Bridezillas*," his father helpfully added.

"Ah, that's the one. Anyway, the perfect *this*, the perfect *that*. Everything delightful for the wedding day. All that money! And then before you know it, bang!" She clapped her hands together and then separated them. "Divorce. Don't worry too much about the wedding day, I say. All you need is the priest, and your family."

Adam stiffened. "Mom, I told you there wasn't time to get the church. We want to get married right away so we're doing it at City Hall."

"Yes, love won't wait. I remember that." She slid a loving gaze at his father. "But you can always do the church wedding later. After the baby."

Adam winced and rubbed the back of his neck.

When he turned to Stacy, she slid him a look that clearly stated he had better sleep with his eyes open tonight.

Even all the brightly lit boats in the Christmas float-boat snowflake parade couldn't distract Stacy from tonight's dinner. Clearly, Adam's mother believed them to be in love. She had no idea that this marriage was a matter of convenience. *And a church wedding!* No, no, that wouldn't happen. Stacy couldn't marry a man who didn't love her, not in a church where *God* would be watching. He might smite them both.

All four of them walked outside together to watch the parade, so she had no time to ask Adam exactly what he'd told his parents. Thankfully, he hadn't told them the truth. Fine with her. But now she wondered if she was supposed to act being in love with Adam. He could have given her a heads-up. Again, he held her hand as they walked, but that had become commonplace. He'd desensitized her to this. It seemed natural now that they would hold hands, because hey, they were in this together. Friends and partners.

Because she liked Adam. Hard not to. In fact, she possibly liked him *too* much. It was important to be cautious and not to invest too much of her emotions in him. At the same time, she worried *he'd* already invested himself too much in their little family. He seemed happy and excited, for which she was grateful. She'd obviously done the right thing to stay. But she was here to help pull him out of his horrible despair, not to hand him yet another loss when they divorced.

He could fool himself into thinking that they'd make a go out of this marriage for the sake of their baby. But she understood on a bone-deep level that Adam's heart wasn't available. He was still grieving his first wife and Stacy wouldn't be in a competition for Adam's heart. She had a baby to raise. And she refused to get herself tied up in knots over a man.

Been there, done that.

"Uncle Adam, there's the Santa boat!" Adam's nephew, Oscar, pointed.

"Pretty cool," Adam said.

And indeed, there was the "real" Santa. Definitely not Max, but a rather short, stout man with a potbelly stomach much like the real deal.

Adam's sister, her husband and their two kids had joined them after dinner for the float-boat parade. Stacy liked Bianca almost immediately. Like Adam, she had gorgeous dark hair and matching eyes. She was sweet and not as outgoing and talkative as her mother. She seemed to take after her father, a man of few words. Her husband, Neal, was the patron saint of patience. He must have told Oscar that he couldn't have any more cotton candy approximately one thousand times. But yet he kept asking. Their little girl, Amber, was simply adorable. She was a toddler, while Oscar was around six or seven, and her favorite word seemed to be *mine*.

"That's where all the lights went," Adam whispered in her ear. "I didn't stand a chance."

A tingle went down her spine at the feel of his warm breath.

Indeed, every boat floated by decorated with colorful bright lights, which lit up the night sky. Some were blinking in patterns. Other boats were filled with flashing stars, wrapped presents, a tiny sleigh, plastic reindeer and trees. Another was filled with characters from *The Nightmare Before Christmas*. A Texas-themed boat sailed by complete with a large lone star blinking brightly enough to be seen from outer space.

There seemed to be a float for everyone, and all glided slowly by to waves and cheers from the audience.

"I'll see you two at the wedding," Bianca said when the parade ended. "These kids have to get to bed."

Adam bent low to engage in a complicated sequence of a handshake/fist bump with Oscar. Since they were all staying at the same hotel, Bianca took her parents back in their car rental. That left Stacy and Adam alone for the first time in hours.

Once they'd walked back to his truck and he'd buckled himself in, he slid her a slow smile and shrugged. "That's the family. Don't blame me, I had no choice in the matter."

"They're wonderful people."

"I don't know if I'd go *that* far." He started the truck and drove them out of the parking lot.

She couldn't believe he thought he'd get away with this. "Oh, Adam. What have you done?"

"Don't worry. Forget about the church wedding."

"I already have, but your poor mother. Do they...?" She studied her hands so she wouldn't have to look at him. "Do they think we're in love? What did you tell them?"

"I told them we'd been dating for a few months before we got serious."

"Adam! That's a lie."

"It's a white lie. You didn't want me to tell them how we really met, did you? What did you tell *your* mother?"

"Well... I'm glad you didn't tell your parents, but I told my mother the honest truth."

"What?" Adam nearly missed a red light and when he came to a sudden stop, he gripped Stacy's shoulder protectively.

She glanced at his hand on her shoulder, surprised by both the quick reflex and rare flash of emotion. "I told you, I'm close to my mother. I tell her everything. We have no secrets."

Adam shook his head. "What must she think of me."

"Are you kidding? She thinks you're a red-blooded

American male. And she *knows* who I am. She trusts you because she trusts me."

"Um, that's not how this works."

And for the first time since she'd met the man, Stacy saw the hint of frustration in his dark eyes. They were darker than normal, his jaw tight, his knuckles nearly white as he gripped the steering wheel.

"You didn't want me to tell my parents how we met, but it was okay to tell your *mother*?"

"Um…when you put it that way… Listen, I never thought I'd *see* you again. I just… I told my mother before I even came out here to see you. Right after I found out about the pregnancy, before I knew anything else. Or whether I'd even…you know…" Her voice petered out, having reached the end of her ridiculous defense.

Your Honor, I plead the Fifth Amendment and throw myself on the mercy of the court.

"Okay, yeah, I guess I can see the difference. But damn, I am not happy about this news." As the light changed, he shook his head. "I'm not angry. This isn't worth getting mad about."

It was as if he was talking to himself, calming down, but she appreciated witnessing this side of Adam. Real. Not perfect. He'd been so incredibly accommodating and good to her that she wondered when she'd see the real him. Aside from his emotional pain, which he'd obviously wrapped back up and put away most days, she didn't see much of who he was.

Against her instincts of self-preservation, Stacy had to disagree. "Actually, you have every right to be angry. It's not fair of me to want to look like a saint while I made you look like a sinner."

"You did that for both of us. Neither one of us are saints. Clearly."

"Honestly, I didn't think you would mind. I mean, doesn't that speak to your manhood? You easily picked up a stranger because you're so handsome and, you know, manly."

Manhood and manly. Boy, wasn't she a first-class writer? No doubt about it, the baby was already using some of her brain cells.

"You didn't think I'd mind that your *mother* knew we went to bed together and had a night of hot sex?"

"Gosh, I didn't give her any of the *details*."

He snorted. "Thanks for that."

They reached the house. Adam pulled into the driveway and shut off the truck.

"I don't want you to hold back your feelings from me." Stacy bit her lower lip, not making a move to get out. "If you're angry and frustrated, that's okay. I'm not an easy person to live with, I know. And I can be demanding, inconsiderate, and now that I'm hormonal, um, somewhat unreasonable. I guess."

In his seat, he shifted and turned to her. "Can I touch your stomach?"

"You want to touch my stomach?" This was not at all what she'd expected him to say.

He gave her a slow smile. "Make up for your incredible lapse in judgment. I want to touch my baby. I'll forgive all."

She took his large hand and placed it on her belly.

This was not something that a husband, fiancé and expectant father would normally have to ask. Once again, she was struck with the oddity of their situation. She'd never imagined that her first baby, her first marriage, would start off this way. With a stranger that she was getting to know more every day. This was a good thing. She had to know the father of her child. Assure herself she was doing the right thing.

Adam's warm hand settled on her stomach. This made the second time he'd touched her so close to the part of her anatomy that caused this situation in the first place. It disturbed her that the small touch sent heat spiraling through her.

"What does it feel like when she moves?"

"I don't think you'll feel it. It's small, like a flutter. Kind of like butterfly wings."

When Adam met her gaze, hand on her stomach, his eyes shimmered with tenderness. The heat surged deeper, stronger, and tugged at the part of her she'd sworn wouldn't get involved.

She'd told herself that Adam's heart wasn't available.

But maybe it was hers.

Chapter Twelve

Wedding day arrived, and Stacy tried on the dress she'd ordered from an online vendor that had shipped it faster than she could make it to the bathroom these days. It was off-white, with an empire waist that nicely camouflaged her expanding belly. Floor-length, with a full skirt that flowed around her legs, it had the added benefit that Stacy could get away with wearing flats. She was already tall at five-nine and rarely wore heels except for special occasions. This *was* a special occasion, but she had already conceded to low heels.

Almost overnight, her stomach popped out. She now had a little "beer" belly in addition to the ex-panding waistline.

So time to face facts. It was official. She was the *matronly* bride. The Madonna.

"You look gorgeous," Grace now said.

She'd managed to get a room at the same hotel in Houston where Stacy's mother would be staying. It was so good to see a friendly face that Stacy felt far more at ease about today than she'd expected.

"And don't forget matronly. I look *matronly*."

"You barely look pregnant. Plus-sized model, that's what you look like. Tall. Curvy."

"I was already *curvy*." She shimmied off the dress, keeping the slip on.

Grace squealed. "Oh, my gosh, look at your cute little baby bump!"

Stacy turned to her side and couldn't help but smile. "Making her presence known."

"She's still itty-bitty, though."

"Not for long."

"Well, I can't wait to meet her. And Adam." Grace hung the dress and smoothed down the skirt. "Where is he, by the way?"

"He's picking up my mother at the airport."

"*That* should be an interesting car ride."

It would be one awkward car ride, but Adam could handle it. Navy SEAL and all. He'd faced worse and it wasn't Stacy's fault that her mother's flight had been canceled and then later delayed leaving Chicago's O'Hare. She was supposed to have arrived earlier, when Stacy had more time to pick her up.

"It's nice that we're having an actual wedding, and not just a come-as-you-are ceremony."

"Adam's friends put this together, and his family wanted to come."

"Well, I'm glad. This is your first marriage, Stacy, no matter the reason. It should be a special day you'll always remember."

"Right. And I'll have photos to show our baby. We can pretend for her sake that we loved each other at one time."

Grace frowned. "You could still grow to love him, you know."

"I can't love someone I essentially don't know. He's holding something back and I can feel it. It's like he walks on eggshells around me. I'm telling you, it's not *normal*."

"He lost someone."

"It's more than that. He's hard on himself, as if he caused it or something."

"What? He didn't, did he?" Grace clutched her chest.

"No," Stacy chuckled. "Are you worried I'm marrying the villain from one of my books? She died in an IED explosion, while working for Doctors Without Borders."

Grace's expression told Stacy that she thought of this in the same way. Adam and his wife were the perfect couple. He was a hero, and she was a heroine who'd lost her life attending to those who were injured.

Stacy smirked. "I know. His first wife was a doctor, his second writes thrillers. What a comparison, right?"

"Don't do that to yourself. You have value, no matter what you do for a living."

"Oh, I know. I'm very different from his first wife, that's all. About as different as two people can get."

"Have you…talked much about her?"

"No, he's very closed off about it. Said he's moving on and wishes everyone would let him. But I've seen him when he stares off into space like he's remembering something painful. He's hurting, and I want to fix this for him."

"Uh-huh." Grace nodded, crossing her arms. "Some people are caregivers in the field, and some people help in their own backyard. Do you ever think that you were possibly attracted to Daniel because he was hurting, too, and you wanted to fix him?"

"No, it's not the same at all."

"Maybe it's a little bit the same."

Stacy had never considered this, but it was true that when she'd first met Daniel, they'd talked a lot about the pain of his divorce. She thought she'd helped him move on. Big mistake, that one.

The doorbell rang and Stacy motioned for Grace to open the front door. "That will be Valerie and Ava, coming over to help."

She'd already told Grace about the fiancées of Adam's closest friends.

"You look gorgeous," Valerie said, after Grace had led the way into the bedroom, where she'd set up.

"Wait until you see the dress." Grace elbowed Stacy.

"Goodness, he hasn't changed much about this room, has he?" Ava glanced around and chuckled.

"Yeah, he told me there hadn't been time to *redecorate*. But it's just me in here, so I appreciate the feminine touches."

If this knowledge was a surprise to them, they didn't give anything away. They'd passed the spare room, where Adam kept his rolled-up sleeping bag and pillow. Clearly, they didn't sleep together. But Adam would have likely told his close friends the truth about their arrangement. She had the feeling the men kept few secrets from their fiancées.

"I don't plan on wearing a lot of makeup today, just to be clear," Stacy told the women. "You could just help me with the hairdo."

She thought it was kind of them to offer to help and seemed like an easy way for Adam's friends to be involved. Until their expectant faces had asked whether they could come help her get ready, she hadn't thought she'd do anything more special than the dress. She wasn't going to go along with anything too dramatic or elegant. The ladies glammed out far more than Stacy did. Ava looked a little like a young Grace Kelly, the movie star of 1950s movies. And Valerie reminded her a little of Meghan Markle. Stacy wasn't sure they'd understand her style.

But she'd always worn the barest makeup. A little mascara, some blush. No fuss, no muss. That was her style.

But when Ava pulled a tiara out of her tote bag, Stacy's no-fuss attitude took a flight to Poughkeepsie, New York, or whatever city and state was farthest from Texas.

"I wear this on my birthday every year," Ava gushed. "Since you don't have a veil, this would be perfect. It could also be your something borrowed!"

"Gor-geous!" Grace said in a singsong and clapped.

"A tiara?" Stacy resisted snatching it out of Ava's hands and placing it on her head, where she'd wear it for the rest of her natural life. A tiara!

"Let's see what it looks like," Valerie said as she fussed with Stacy's hair.

Valerie curled the ends, then pinned up some of the sides, letting ringlets fall loose. The moment the small crown was placed on her head, Stacy knew it was right. Perfect. This was *her* day, after all. The one concession to making the day a smidgen of what she'd always dreamed of as a little girl. Her special wedding-day tiara and all.

It wasn't happening in a church, as she'd once imagined…but would *not* tell Mrs. Cruz. It wasn't happening with a man she adored, and who adored her back. But nevertheless, her little baby bump made up for all she'd miss.

And so would this tiara.

* * *

It turned out that the inside of city hall was almost obscenely beautiful. A grand staircase, reminding Stacy of the one in a movie featuring a beauty and a beast, was the focal point as one walked through the double glass doors. The inside colors were white and gold, and the vaulted ceiling gave the sensation of being inside a cathedral. There were Roman-style pillars and balconies on the second floor, and windows that allowed bright rays of sunshine to spill in.

"Oh, my," Stacy's mother said from beside her. She hadn't really let go of Stacy since arriving. "I certainly didn't expect this."

"Neither did I." Stacy stared around in awe.

"Charming believes in preserving our history, and this building has been here since the town was founded. It's survived *two* hurricanes. There have been a few minor improvements here and there, but it's safe to say our founders had lofty hopes for Charming," Ava said, gesturing around. "It never worked out to be quite the tourist mecca they'd imagined, but we do okay."

Stacy, her mother and Adam followed Ava and Max as they made their way up the staircase to one of the judges' offices. Valerie, Cole and the rest brought up the rear, stopping to take photos along the way.

"My writer's heart is overflowing," Grace said, taking a photo from the top of the staircase. "This is so romantic."

Upstairs, the clerk's offices were dark wood doors

that *smelled* old. At the entrance, Stacy turned back to view the group. Adam's family and friends made up three-fourths of those attending their little ceremony.

"I'm sorry, but most of you will have to wait outside." Ava turned to the group. "We just need Stacy, Adam and two witnesses to sign the official marriage license."

"I'm a witness," offered Stacy's mother, still hanging tight to Stacy's arm.

"So am I!" Adam's mother elbowed her way to the front.

"Mom," Stacy whispered. "Do you think you could let go of me long enough that I could get married?"

Two seconds after Mom withdrew the death grip on Stacy's arm, Adam was beside her. He confidently took her hand and squeezed it. She looked up at him, and really *saw* him for the first time that day. *Noticed* him. He'd chosen a suit and tie that matched his dark coloring and looked breathtakingly handsome. Stacy wouldn't have blamed him if he'd worn slacks and a nice shirt, but he'd gone all out. And, dear Lord above, he smelled wonderful.

I'm about to get married to this gorgeous man. Is this my life?

"Sign here, please." The clerk pointed to the certificate.

"Second thoughts?" Stacy joked. "Get out now while you still can."

"Not on your life." Adam leaned forward and signed the document.

Then, just outside the judge's chambers, with family and friends behind them, a few words were exchanged that changed everything.

And Stacy Hartsell became Stacy Cruz.

For the second time in his life, Adam was a married man.

But this time, he wasn't nervous at all. He looked at Stacy, found his center and had no doubts. Maybe because he was older, or because he'd be a father, but this time his wedding day felt markedly different. It wasn't until Ava asked them to please pose for a few photos at the top of the staircase that Adam remembered similar photos taken. It felt as though that day had happened to a different person. He briefly thought of Mandy then, but this time without guilt pressing down and threatening to derail him. Without pain slicing through him. She was now a nice memory of a different time in his life.

Now, there was Stacy, and their baby, and they filled all the empty grooves and cracks in his soul. They'd put him back together. She was almost incomparably beautiful today. He'd never understand how or why she went home with him that night.

Ava didn't have to pose them. No one did, because this time there was no professional photographer to arrange them. This time, Adam reached for his wife and pulled her back to his front, his arm circling just above her baby bump. She leaned back her head and it touched his shoulder.

"Aw," Ava said. "Perfect. Just perfect."

"Stay like that," Valerie ordered, holding up one hand with a *stop* gesture, whipping out her phone with the other one.

Then everyone took out their phones and clicked away. Even Cole and Max. More photos were taken with Stacy and Adam at the balcony holding hands, then walking down one of the long corridors arm in arm, and finally, looking out one of the windows as a beam of sunlight showered over them.

Later, he figured, he'd look back on these photos and regret only one thing.

They didn't kiss once. But how he wanted to kiss her. In the same way he'd pulled her to him, he wanted to get her in a lip-lock she couldn't escape. He'd decided not to push his luck. She'd married him. If anything more were ever to materialize, he'd be the luckiest man alive. But it would be entirely up to her.

Stacy would have to fall in love with him because she wouldn't have a real marriage any other way. He understood more than she realized, but he'd already been half in love with her when she showed up announcing she'd be having his baby. It wouldn't be difficult to fall the rest of the way, but he'd be lying to say that he wasn't holding back. He'd already been through enough loss and if he fell the rest of the way for Stacy, and she left him as planned, he wasn't sure he could ever come back from that.

Cole had been right. It was up to Adam to guard his heart.

"Shouldn't we get to the reception now?" Stacy's mother said.

"Oh, I guess we should!" Grace laughed and glanced at her phone. "I think I have enough photos."

At that moment Adam glanced around and realized that his friends and family had all gone ahead.

"Looks like we're the last few left here." He led the way out, holding open doors.

Stacy's mother, Regina, was not a big fan of his. He could hardly blame her, with her wealth of knowledge about him. On the way from the airport to Charming, she'd interrogated him. And he wasn't using the term lightly, either, having been well versed in the technique. He halfway expected her to shine a bright light on him.

"Any drug problems, Adam?" she'd asked, then continued with a litany of questions.

"Do you drink?

"I understand you're a former Navy SEAL. You don't plan on reupping again, do you?

"I'm very sorry to hear about your late wife. How long did your first marriage last?

"How long have your parents been married? Any brothers or sisters? Have any of them ever been in jail?

"Have you ever served time?"

Anyone else would get *the look* he'd perfected over years of training and missions. The *look* said,

"You are now close to death. Back off." But first, no woman ever got *the look* out of him. Second, this was Stacy's mother and as such would be treated with the proper reverence. Even if she stepped on his last nerve. He reminded himself that she believed him to be the kind of man who trolled bars looking for beautiful women. The kind of man who took a woman home so he could proceed to have sex, with plans to never see her again. Far from the man he was.

But no amount of smoothness on his part would fix this. Regina's mind was made up about him, and clearly, she put her daughter first. Once he'd seen them together, it became apparent that Stacy's mother was almost unnaturally attached to her. Almost…needy.

Realizing that mothers and daughters had a special connection, he'd chosen not to be greedy, or worried. Still, he understood with a biting certainty that if Stacy didn't stay with him, Regina would have a lot to do with it. Clearly, they'd had other plans before he'd entered the picture. They were extremely close, and Stacy had planned to raise her child alongside her mother with the support she'd need. He'd interfered, and Regina couldn't be happy about that, even if she understood the reasoning behind marrying Stacy. Stacy's mother thought this only had to do with the health insurance.

But Adam wasn't sure it had ever been only the insurance. Not for him. That had been his ace and he'd used it. But he'd wanted Stacy and their baby in his life from the moment he'd heard the news.

When they arrived at the lighthouse, the party was already in full swing. Guests were spilling out of the house onto the beach. Adam spotted Bianca and Neal walking along the shoreline, their kids running ahead of them. Torchlights were lit and stuck into the ground at strategic places around a circle of lawn chairs.

Valerie and Cole greeted them as they walked inside to cheers from their few guests. There was an amazing array of dishes spread over the counter in the kitchen. Everything from platters of chicken to salads, cakes and pies.

"You didn't have to go to this much trouble," Stacy said to Valerie, giving her a quick hug.

"No big deal. We all brought a dish. Potluck style." Valerie pointed to the guests, which included her grandmother, Patsy Villanueva.

The feisty senior citizen had switched from a walker to a cane in the last couple of weeks and seemed to be doing much better after her hip surgery.

"Adam!" Patsy opened her arms and he bent low to hug her. "We haven't known each other for long, but I'm a big fan of love, as you will soon hear all about."

"My grandmother has written you two a poem she'd like to recite," Valerie said, and her cheeks pinked.

"It's my wedding gift to you. No need to thank

me! Let me meet this lovely wife of yours." Patsy shuffled past him to Stacy. "My dear, aren't you beautiful? How far along are you?"

"About twenty weeks," Stacy said.

"I once wrote a poem about pregnancy, but no one liked it." With true skill, Patsy used her cane like a shepherd's staff to point, and encouraged Stacy to follow her farther into the living room.

The rest of the members of the Almost Dead Poet Society were lounging on the couch, including Susannah.

"Hey."

Adam turned to see Cole, grinning as he brandished two cigars. Max, next to him, already held one in his hand.

"Step into my office." Cole walked toward the glass sliders leading to the beach cove in the back.

Adam glanced back to see that Stacy, Grace and Regina were occupied chatting with Mrs. Villanueva and her friends. He shrugged off his jacket and followed his friends outside into the winter night.

At the edge of the surf, Max lit them up with a single match. "Congratulations."

"Thank you." Adam took a big drag and watched the smoke billow. "I never thought this could happen to me. Never thought I'd get married again."

"A baby sure makes a family happy." Cole sounded wistful. His own mother had passed several years ago and would never meet Cole and Valerie's future children.

"It's not just the baby," Adam said. "It's Stacy. I can't separate the two. It's her and the baby. I need them both."

"You deserve this more than anyone, Adam." Cole clapped him on the back.

"So…she's staying?" Max asked. "Because, you know, you just got here."

"Don't worry. You need me, and I'm not taking off on you geniuses. Just like you wanted, I'm buying in to the bar."

"No one wanted to force your hand on this," Cole said. "We just…wanted you to put down roots. Thought it might be time."

A ripple of tension rolled through Adam. He knew where this was going. His buddies thought he'd been shiftless and aimless for too long. They were probably concerned that he wouldn't be able to follow through with his commitment to Stacy. And he had to admit to himself that for a long while after he'd left the service, he hadn't known what he would do next, or how he'd live the rest of his life. But after the night he'd met Stacy, he'd never been quite the same. Since then, something nameless had been brooding inside of him, like a caged animal that wanted out. For too long he'd confined himself to existing. Not living.

"I haven't had much direction, I admit. But I do now. I only needed some time to clear my head."

"Yeah." Cole flicked an ash from the cigar, then cleared his throat. "I also know about grief. It's hard to get through it."

"There's no comparison. You didn't cause your mother's cancer."

"And you didn't cause Mandy's death, no matter how much you tell yourself you should have stopped her from getting into the middle of that…mess."

"I understand this and I've accepted it. There wasn't anything I could have done. But I'll damn well bet the last words you said to your mother weren't ugly. They weren't words you wished you could obliterate."

"No, not words. But I wasn't there when she got sick, because I was on the other side of the world saving someone else's ass. Not here with her when she needed me the most. And *that* stayed with me for a long time."

Feeling Cole's pain more than he wanted to, Adam placed a hand over his shoulder. "You managed to let it go."

"Because holding on to guilt won't do a damn thing for you. It's a useless emotion. I have regrets, sure, but my mother *knew* I loved her. And so did Mandy. She knew. You gotta let it go."

"You're right. She'd forgive me. I have to find a way to forgive myself."

Chapter Thirteen

"And never, ever, go to bed angry," Mrs. Villanueva said to Stacy, shaking a finger.

"That's another good one," Lois said. "You will, of course, get mad at each other but just don't let it fester."

But Stacy didn't fester—instead, she was skilled at avoidance. She had a fairly good disappearing act when someone got too upset with her. She detested conflict of any kind, hence her issues with her mother. But she couldn't picture ever working up a good "mad" for Adam. And for his part, he'd been frustrated with her...twice. Even in these upsetting circumstances, he'd never been angry with her. Either way, she loved that these kind people thought she had a real marriage. Their advice was well meant. She'd be co-parenting with Adam for many years. These were lessons she would still be able to use.

"Forgiveness is a wonderful part of marriage," added Mr. Finch. "And it goes both ways, ladies."

Tonight, Stacy had met the rest of the members of the Almost Dead Poet Society. Etta Mae Virgil, Mrs. Villanueva and Lois. They were lovely people, and even her mother seemed to enjoy talking to them. She had been sitting between Lois and Etta Mae, deep in animated conversation about the movie version of *Little Women*.

Stacy had to find a few minutes to take her mother aside and talk to her privately. She was not looking forward to this because her mother wouldn't be happy. There was so much to explain, such as why she felt compelled to stay with Adam and not return to Chicago right away. Her mother had simply assumed that Stacy would be coming back after the marriage and get her medical care at a local VA in Chicago. It was what she'd wanted Stacy to do, and she hadn't told her other otherwise. Mom wouldn't take the news well. Almost their entire lives, it had been just the three of them—Mom, Nana and Stacy. There had never been a father figure in the picture, and that had worked out just fine with Stacy. All three were working women, all of them independent and self-made. But her mother hadn't approved when Stacy moved to Montana to get away from Daniel and Dominique.

"Chicago is a big enough city for the three of you!" she'd said. "Don't let them chase you out of here."

Stacy never told her mother that when the opportunity to strike out on her own presented itself, she'd wanted to take it and run. She'd felt guilt leaving her mother, because by then it was just the two of them, with Nana gone. Stacy lived nearby and checked in with her mother daily. She found it natural to tell her mother everything, until she met Grace, who expressed shock at the openness of Stacy's relationship with her mother.

The word *boundaries* had been brought up and Stacy had to admit that she'd had few with her mother. Maybe not such a good thing.

Grace pulled Stacy aside. "Oh, my Lord, Stacy, you never mentioned Adam is *gorgeous*."

"I didn't?"

"Well, hell's bells, girl! No wonder you married him. I would marry him if he'd have me. He's got that whole Heathcliff thing going on." She gestured, sweeping a hand through the air. "They invented the phrase 'tall, dark, and handsome' for him."

"Okay, Grace. Calm down." Stacy laughed. "Remember this is a marriage of convenience. Health insurance. I'm carrying his child. That's the only reason he married me."

Grace looked deflated, like someone had let all her air out. "Are you sure?"

Stacy leaned in and whispered, "He hasn't even tried anything with me. Not a hint of desire."

"Oh." She patted Stacy's back. "I'm sorry, honey."

"That's okay. I don't have time to fall in love. I have a book to write, and a baby to gestate." She patted her belly. "I'm a little busy here."

"There you go. Well, it would have been nice. Nothing works out perfectly except in my books. At least you'll be sure to have a beautiful baby." Grace's eyes turned to the beach cove outside, and Stacy followed her gaze.

There stood Adam, Cole and Max, their backs to them as they faced the ocean. Outside, a ray of moonlight glinted off Adam's dark hair. He was slightly taller than Cole and Max, and around them, he had a commanding presence. Clearly, the men respected him. Cole had admitted that he owed Adam his life. Stacy wanted to know more, but the way Adam had shut down meant she wouldn't bring it up again anytime soon.

He'd tell her everything, sooner or later, and she'd strive to be that soft place for him to fall.

"Stacy, honey," her mother said, interrupting her thoughts. "Your new friends are so kind. They invited me to a poetry reading. That would have been nice, but I had to remind them that we're leaving in a couple of days. Did you make your airline reservations yet?"

"Excuse me," Grace said, and stepped away to join the others by the snack table.

"Mom, I'm...um, we need to talk." Stacy led her

mother outside, just as Cole, Max and Adam were coming inside.

As Adam approached, he smiled, then brushed her hand with his fingers when he walked past her. It was just the kind of tender gesture a good man would give his wife and the mother of his child. Sweet and affectionate. Friendly. Chaste. Sometimes she had the distinct feeling that Adam was going through the motions, like he had a script to follow. Dutiful husband and future father.

Stacy walked her mother far enough away from everyone lingering outside for some privacy.

"What is it? Is it the baby? Is something wrong?" Mom held a hand to her throat.

"No. I've just made a decision I'm afraid you won't like. I'm staying here with Adam. At least until after the baby is born."

"Stacy! Why would you want to do that?"

For many reasons. Adam needed her, and for now she thought maybe she needed him a little, too. He took care of her like no one ever had before. And the thought of him following her to Chicago, and leaving all this support he had behind... Well, she couldn't do that to a man obviously struggling.

"I like it here."

"It's beautiful, true, but it's *Texas*. You're going to *hate* the heat and humidity in the summer. And you'll be so far away from me!"

"Closer than I was in Montana." Stacy shrugged.

"Montana was to have been temporary, and I didn't like that, either."

"It's just that Adam will move to Chicago if I do, and I can't let him do that."

"Why not? That sounds like the perfect solution."

"I can't explain it, but Adam…needs to be here with his close friends. They all served together, and I can tell they're close. They're his support system."

"And I'm yours!"

This was the tough part and Stacy sucked in a breath and slowly let it out. "I'm grateful for that, because I'm never going to stop asking for your advice. Especially after the baby comes. I'll have a dozen questions. You're my mother and I love and respect you. But… I—I think Adam is going to be my support system from now on."

"Adam?"

"He's the father of my child and he will *always* be the father. No matter what, we're linked together. We'll have to co-parent for the next eighteen years. We will always be a family, one way or another."

"If you're lucky, and that's a big *if.* You don't think your father said the same thing to me?" Her eyes narrowed.

"Okay, Mom, look, I don't want to do this right now. This is a party." Her heart rate speeding up and her mouth drying, she glanced around, now hoping someone would walk up and *interrupt* them. "I just wanted to tell you why I'm not making a reservation."

Mom jabbed her finger in the air. "You need to

hear this. Some fathers have the best of intentions, but raising a baby is a major overhaul to anyone's existence. A lot of men just can't hang in there with all the life changes."

"That's not Adam." Stacy shook her head. "You don't know him."

"And neither do *you*. Can you tell me you know *everything* about this man who will be your baby's father?"

"Um…"

"Didn't you say that you couldn't find him because he'd suddenly picked up and moved? Didn't you find out that he's had a series of dead-end jobs and a nomad kind of existence?"

"Yes, but…"

"I don't want you to get hurt again counting on a man when you should be responsible for your own happiness."

"I *am* responsible for my own happiness."

"Are you?" Mom crossed her arms and puckered her lips.

When had her mother become such a judgmental, stuck-up, self-righteous and bitter woman? Had she always been like this? Was Stacy only now having her eyes opened to the facts? But, no, she hadn't always been this bad. She'd gotten worse since Stacy left Chicago. She recognized the signs of someone desperately trying to hang on to what they were terrified of losing.

Grace had been right. Stacy and her mother had

no boundaries. They were codependent, stuck in a pattern they'd had for years of overreliance on each other. When they'd only had each other as Stacy grew up, it made sense. But somewhere along the line Stacy failed to establish healthy boundaries. How well she remembered leaving for college, which, due to her mother's separation anxiety, had been right in Chicago. Still, she'd lived on campus and guilt forced her to call her mother daily.

Now, she tugged on her mother's hand. "This doesn't mean we won't see each other, Mom. And we'll talk every day."

"And I'll be there for you when this doesn't work out with Adam."

But the words, if they were meant to be soothing at all, were said with such a bite of anger that Stacy's eyes stung with tears.

"It almost sounds like you wish he *would* walk away from his child, and that can't be what you want."

"Of course not." She shook her head. "But it's likely what will happen, honey. You need to face it. You'll do what you always do. Leave at the first sign of trouble, but it won't be as easy to do when you're married and pregnant. Before long you'll feel dependent on him. Besides, this is temporary. Don't get all romantic about it just because he's good-looking."

"He's *good* to me," Stacy said. "Better than anyone has been for a long time."

"Stacy." The deep voice behind her could belong

to no one other than Adam. When she turned, he stood a few feet behind her. His brow furrowed in obvious concern. "Everything okay?"

She wiped away the single tear her mother's callous words caused. "I'm fine."

Adam did not look convinced as he took another step toward her. "Ava wants us to dance."

"Like at a real wedding?" her mother quipped.

"This *is* a real wedding," Adam said sternly.

His tone said the subject was closed, and it was also the angriest she'd ever heard him. He offered his hand to Stacy, holding it out and meeting her gaze, silently willing her to take it.

She did, then turned to her mother. "I'll see you in there."

Adam had interrupted a tense exchange between Stacy and her mother. There was no hiding the glint of tears in Stacy's eyes. He understood the tears of a woman by now, and these were hurt tears, not I'm-going-to-miss-you tears. The realization that her mother had caused them was difficult to accept.

There was a tension thick in the air between these two women. He didn't know what had happened, but he wanted it to stop. Her crack about their wedding was unacceptable and Adam had never been one to barter for peace to avoid conflict. He always faced conflict head-on and dealt with it. It had managed to land him in some tight situations, but hell, some fights had to be won.

When they crossed the threshold into the open lower room of the house, the mood shifted and changed. Ava, Max, Valerie, Cole and all their friends turned expectant smiles in their direction.

"Tennessee Whiskey" by Chris Stapleton began to play through the surround-sound speakers. When Ava had asked him for any special song choices, he'd mentioned this song because it had been playing in the background the night he and Stacy met. He remembered her chatting away about Chicago, while she drove him to distraction with her wicked laugh. Her shimmering eyes had been filled with intelligence and humor.

He'd been moved by the bluesy song about a man who'd been rescued from too much drinking by a woman who tasted as sweet as strawberry wine. Then he'd asked Stacy to dance because it seemed like the thing to do. And she'd danced with him for the first and only time until this moment.

"You remembered." Stacy looked up at him, a gleam in her eyes, and until now he wasn't sure that she would, too.

"Of course. I just didn't know if you would." He held out his hand for her to join him in the middle of the room.

She did, winding her hands around his neck and smiling up at him. He pulled her close, resting his hands low on the curve of her back. Though he'd forgotten *how* to dance, none of that seemed to matter. Stacy met his gaze and didn't look away for several minutes. He lowered his head and let his lips hover near hers, the sweet pulsations of desire enough. For now.

This made the closest he'd ever come to kissing anyone without actually touching lips.

After the song and ensuing applause, everyone else joined them on the "dance floor." Faster music took over, with songs like "Tequila," which began to suggest a theme. There were a few people drinking though not Adam, or Stacy, naturally. Adam danced with Bianca, and Neal danced with Stacy. Then Valerie and Cole. Ava, apparently known for dancing on tables, hopped up on a coffee table with Max. Max, for his part, did the expert eighth-grade shuffle, "dancing" by hanging on to Ava's behind. But, hey, he looked good while doing so. No one rocked a suit like Max Del Toro.

His parents were in the middle of this fray, and so was Grace. But Adam hadn't spotted Regina in a while.

He'd just finished dancing the "Macarena" with Oscar when he saw Stacy, shaking her head to another dance with Cole. Looking flushed, she wandered up the winding staircase to the second level.

What was wrong with him, having a good time dancing and ignoring his bride? Of course, she was tired. This had been a long day for him, so he couldn't imagine how *she* must feel.

He bounded up the steps after her, finding her on the deck, where there was an old-fashioned telescope, like the kind a lighthouse attendant would have used in days of old to find and identify lost ships, leading them home. He remembered the first time he'd seen it, marveling at the history. Stacy seemed equally enthralled, having not even heard him come up behind her. She was peeking through the scope, bent low, and in her wedding dress she made an interesting picture.

"Bride searches for groom lost at sea?"

She startled and whipped around to face him. "This is so cool."

"It is."

"I'm sorry that I don't write books about pirates. Maybe I should try."

"Yeah. Why not?"

She wrapped her arms around her waist. "The stars are so bright tonight."

He stepped into her and draped his arm around her shoulder. "Are you cold?"

"Aren't you? Oh, never mind." She shook her head, smiling. "Navy SEAL."

"It's true, I think I developed a high tolerance for the cold. And the heat." He did not want to think of those missions right now. Of all those times far from home, fighting just to stay alive.

He'd done his job and moved on. "We should go. You look tired."

"I am, a little. Adam, I..." She seemed to hesitate. "This was a nice party. You have great friends."

"They're your friends, too."

They stood there for a few minutes, just listening to the waves crashing on the rocks below. A seagull cawed in the distance. The wind whipped Stacy's long hair in the breeze and that surge of tenderness hit him again.

"There you are!" Valerie clasped her hands together, pleading. "Please, please, come back down before my grandmother comes looking for you up here. God knows she'll crawl up here if she has to."

"Does she need something?" Hand low on Stacy's back, he urged her toward the balcony door.

"Your ears, unfortunately." Valerie sighed. "She and Lois are getting ready to leave with Mr. Finch, and she absolutely insists on giving you the wedding gift she promised. The poem?"

"Ah, yes."

He'd heard a whole lot about this senior-citizen poetry. They were accidental matchmakers far more than they were great laureates. But, hey, it was a small price to pay for this party.

"After that, we're leaving," Adam said. "Stacy is tired."

Downstairs, the music had stopped, and they all gathered near the couch and surrounded Mrs. Villanueva, who stood to recite her poem.

"This is titled, 'Make Love Once a Day' and it's my wish for you, Stacy and Adam, bride and groom."

Adam smothered a smile when Valerie hid her face in the crook of Cole's shoulder.

The poem, which didn't rhyme, talked about the

importance of touching. Of connection. Kisses and long lazy days in bed. Making breakfast and having another round after the meal. At one point, Adam's mother gaped and covered her mouth in disbelief. His father cracked a smile, a rare event. Bianca and Neal could barely contain their wide grins. Valerie now seemed to have disappeared into Cole's neck, who was shaking with silent laughter. Max stood behind Ava, arms around her waist, his head resting in the crook of her shoulder.

The rest of the senior-citizen poets sat silently, thoughtfully nodding at times, supportive in every way. They were the first to clap when, at last, the erotic poetry was finally over.

Adam was dying here. He touched Stacy every chance he had. Hell, he was touching her now. And though she allowed him, she never initiated a thing.

It was as if she'd decided that she would tolerate him for the sake of peace and their baby.

Chapter Fourteen

Mrs. Villanueva was so incredibly sincere about all the sex that she swore was vital to a long-lasting marriage. She obviously had no inhibitions when it came to her poetry, either, reminding Stacy of an earlier time in her own writing. Once, the wretched internal editor sat on her shoulder and criticized everything she wrote, nearly destroying her career before it got off the ground. She admired someone who could be so open, not just about her sexuality, but her wordsmithing. The words weren't perfect, but they were on point. The woman had a fresh voice that could not be contained. Or restrained, much to poor Valerie's despair.

When it was over, Stacy applauded the loudest. So loudly that Adam slid her a curious smile.

"It takes a lot of guts to do something like that," she whispered to him.

"No doubt."

With the party winding down, Bianca and Neal gathered up their kids.

"Welcome to the family," Bianca said, giving Stacy a huge hug. "I'll be in touch. The kids definitely want to meet their little cousin when he or she makes their appearance."

"I'll be back for the baby shower," Adam's mother said. "El Paso is just a quick plane ride away."

In between all the family hugs and goodbyes, Stacy noticed someone notably absent. Her mother hung back. Was she really going to be this immature about the situation? Stacy wished for a family more like Adam's—they simply accepted the choices their children made. They couldn't be happy about an unplanned pregnancy, but they were welcoming Stacy into their family nonetheless and had relieved her concerns.

Adam led her outside, holding her hand as he always seemed to do these days. The sound of the nearby waves was soothing, the air salty and cold and clear. Spectacular stars were spread across the black sky like a carpet.

Yeah, she could get used to this place.

"Honey, thank you for inviting me to your wedding." Grace caught up to Stacy and Adam.

Stacy grabbed her friend in a hug. "Did you really think I'd do this without you?"

"No, because if not for me, you wouldn't even be in this situation. Aren't you glad I do such good research?" Grace glanced over at Adam, who was walking toward the passenger side of the truck, no doubt to hold the door open for Stacy.

"Yes, of course. I hit the jackpot of baby daddies. Who knew?"

"Are you sure that's all there is? I don't know. The way he looks at you…"

"Tender, right?"

"Yes." Grace sighed, her romance-writer heart full, no doubt.

"I *am* the mother of his child. Adam is the kind of good man who appreciates that his baby has taken over my body. That I'm giving him a chance to be a father. That's not a small thing to him and he appreciates me."

"Oh, gosh, there's no way you could ever write romance," Grace said. "You lack imagination."

"Tell me about it."

A few feet away, Stacy's mom walked toward Grace's rental.

"Mom," Stacy called out.

She didn't even turn, and she *had* to have heard Stacy. Unbelievable. "She's giving me the cold shoulder."

"Why?"

"It's the codependency you were talking about. I finally admit it. Maybe we lacked boundaries for too long."

Rolling her eyes, Grace pressed the clicker on her key fob and Stacy's mother opened the passenger door and shut it. "That's something you can both work on."

Stacy vowed to do the work on her end, but if her mother wouldn't cooperate and was going to freeze her out, they wouldn't get very far. Pain sliced through Stacy. This was her wedding day, no matter the reason, and her mother had intentionally tried to ruin her happiness. Simply because she didn't get her way.

"This is what she does. If I don't do what she *thinks* I should, she becomes this immature woman. In two days, she'll probably call me. She'll be needy, and remorseful. Then we'll start all over again, sliding back into old patterns. I'll feel guilty for being a bad daughter and let her back in without putting up those boundaries." Stacy took a deep breath and let it out. "I told her I'm staying in Charming for the remainder of the pregnancy. She thought after I married Adam, I could still go back to Chicago, and get medical care from the VA there."

"Uh-huh. And why exactly have you decided to stay? She's right, you know. All other things being equal." She threw an appreciative gaze toward Adam, now chatting with Max and Cole. "Which, of course, they're not."

Stacy's eyes naturally gravitated toward Adam, too. He had a good, deep laugh, which she didn't hear often enough.

"He needs me to stay. Otherwise, he'd follow me to Chicago. And he needs his friends. He needs to be here."

"I don't blame you for staying. This is my kind of winter. As soon as I get back home, I'll go back to wearing snow boots and parkas." She elbowed Stacy. "Don't worry, I'll talk to your mother."

"It won't do any good, but thank you for trying." Stacy opened her mouth, the closed it. She hesitated for a beat. Then two.

She still hadn't told Grace the whole story. How she'd found the framed wedding photo of Adam and his wife and decided not to pursue their relationship anymore. It had all simply been too embarrassing, but she'd told her mother, after all. And she was going to stop telling her *everything* from this day forward, so help her.

"Um, remember I told you that Adam and I had a one-night stand?"

"Yes, your first one of those, and you swore it would be your last. You're not cut out for that sort of thing, Stacy. You should have known better."

"You don't know the half of it. Here's the thing. I did know better. That's not at all the way we started out, or what I wanted. It wasn't *supposed* to be a one-night stand. *I* made it that way. It was because of something I saw the next morning."

With that, Stacy gave Grace the short version.

Grace's eyes widened, and then her naturally empathetic side rose like a phoenix. "Stacy, you should have told me. I had no idea you'd been dealing with this."

Or not dealing with it.

"It was just too embarrassing. That's why I hesitated to contact him about the baby, too. Talk about overcomplicating the poor man's life. As if he doesn't have enough going on."

"Or it could be this is exactly what he needed."

"I hope so. Unless the stress finally breaks him in two. But I want to help him, and he needs the support system that he has here."

"Don't forget that you need a support system, too."

"He's all that for me and more."

"But that's all about the baby, right?"

"That's all I need, and he's been wonderful. I couldn't ask for a better partner."

"That is *not* all you need!" Grace gripped Stacy's shoulders and gave her a little shake. "You deserve more than that, Stacy. Don't shortchange yourself."

"Some people can have love. I'll take door number two, please, the health insurance."

"You're not *that* jaded, are you?"

"Maybe I am. And the last thing I'm ever going to do again is be any man's second choice."

Yes, logically, she understood that there was no comparison between her previous disaster of an unintentional triangle and this. Poor Mandy could hardly give Stacy any competition. But feelings were a rather strange phenomenon. Stacy couldn't help believing that she'd come in second again.

"And she's still sitting there waiting for you." Stacy hooked a finger in the direction of Grace's rental, changing the subject to an easier one. "Pouting, I'm sure."

Stacy could go over there now, and smooth things over. She'd apologize and explain that she was still trying to figure things out. Tell Mom she'd rethink and maybe come out to Chicago after all. That would be enough to pull her mother out of her funk. Maybe she owed her that, because she'd been a struggling single mother who'd made certain Stacy never wanted for much of anything growing up.

But she'd given in too many times in the past. It had always been Stacy apologizing, Stacy compromising, Stacy always wrong. Her mother had never been wrong in any scenario, which, of course, wasn't possible.

As if fresh off a cocktail of hormones, Stacy was suddenly livid. A hot pang of anger ran through her, making every muscle in her tighten. No, she would not apologize for making this decision. It was the right one, and she'd gone into this marriage with her eyes wide open.

"Tell my mother I said good night, would you?" Stacy gave Grace one last squeeze.

With that, she walked to where Adam was holding the door open, got in the car and didn't look back.

"Are you going straight to bed?" Adam asked as he opened the front door.

"I think I'd better."

They'd been mostly quiet on the ride back to

their home, Stacy fuming about her mother. And, of course, she had no idea what Adam was thinking. She rarely did.

"It was a long day." Adam folded his suit jacket and laid it on the back of the sofa. "You must be exhausted."

He'd loosened his tie and rolled up the sleeves of his white shirt to his elbows. And that unfairly sexy dark stubble dusting his chin and jawline...

"Do you want me to run you a hot bath?"

For the love of all that was holy. He was so damn perfect she wanted to cry.

Why couldn't she have met him at a different time? She'd been in Montana for a while and never met *anyone* like him. And why couldn't she simply have sucked it up, put on her big-girl panties and *asked* him about the photo instead of running away like a scared little girl? Everything might have been different. They could have had the actual start of a real relationship before she found out she was pregnant. Now, she'd never know.

And why, why, oh, why did he have to be so pleasant when she'd disrupted his entire life?

"No, *thank* you," she finally answered.

Instead of a hot bath, which sounded heavenly, she closed the door to her bedroom. And stared at herself in the mirror. Once, she'd been fairly attractive to the opposite sex. Looking back, she'd enjoyed that. Loved watching men trip over themselves trying to get her attention. Daniel had asked her out three times before she'd said yes—the biggest mistake of her life. Should have said no a fourth time.

Right now, she only wanted the attention of one man. She wished Adam would look at her with even the slightest hint of desire in his eyes. If they were going to be married for a while, it would be nice to enjoy regular sex. Even pregnant, she could see the advantages to that. But all she ever saw out of him were hints of the tenderness and affection directed to his offspring, whom she happened to be carrying. For one moment, during their first dance, she thought she'd seen something else. The sweet ache and intensity of hot desire. But he hadn't kissed her. She wondered if he was going through the motions for everyone else's sake. And for hers.

Because listening to "Tennessee Whiskey" had taken her back in time. Back to a night when she'd hoped for something new and sweet in her life. Love, maybe. And she'd wound up with a change, all right, just not at all the kind she'd intended.

"You're ridiculous," she said as she lowered her dress, stepped out of it and hung it up.

She was having a *baby*, a precious child, who would have a wonderful father. He'd care for their daughter. He'd be there for her. It didn't matter that he didn't love the mother of his child—a man like Adam would never let that stand in the way of being a good father. Stacy was so damn lucky. She could have wound up with a different kind of man that night, one who was all about himself. All about his own satisfaction. All about getting his most basic needs met.

You knew better from the moment he spoke to you.

She was a smart and intelligent woman, and she'd read Adam's body language. He spoke with respect and consideration. Maybe she'd done enough writing and observing of human nature over the years. Because she would have never gone home with him without the deep-seated knowledge that he would never hurt her. Tears prickled now and slid down her cheeks. She'd hoped for much more at one time and would now spend her wedding night alone.

Maybe it didn't have to be this way.

Why *should* she be alone when he was in the next room? They could talk about today. Maybe they could make more plans for their baby. A few days ago, he'd asked in passing about a crib. She'd mentioned that it should be in her bedroom and he'd agreed that made sense. A conversation between two friends and roommates. It was fine. Good.

But all she wanted now was for Adam to hold her all night. The slip she'd worn under the wedding dress felt silky and soft, smooth against her bare skin. The urgency rolling through her moved her to act and she padded across the carpet on bare feet.

The door to Adam's bedroom was cracked open. As she watched, he slid off his tie and unbuttoned his shirt, completely unaware of Stacy. Gorgeous, taut, tanned skin peeked from underneath, fully revealed in all its splendor when he shrugged off the shirt. She swallowed hard when he moved to hang it, his back to her now. Muscles bunched—utter male perfection. Sigh. She almost wished for a boy. Amazing genes to pass down.

Yes, that's your daddy. You are welcome, little one.

Lust raged inside her like a gale-force hurricane. She wanted Adam so desperately that she didn't have room for any other thoughts.

"Adam."

He turned, eyebrow quirked, registering surprise.

Maybe because she stood in the door frame of his room, in her slip, eyes probably pinked with tears, his eyes narrowed in concern. "What's wrong?"

"No, I'm fine. Nothing. I…" With effort, she met his eyes. "I can't speak for you, but this is not at all what I'd imagined for my wedding night. Separate bedrooms."

He cocked his head, the barest hint of a smile on his lips.

"And… I really don't want to be alone right now."

She was in his arms before she'd even realized that he'd crossed the room. And, oh, dear heavens, it was *good* to be held like this. This was the physical manifestation of the way he'd taken care of her since the day she'd arrived. Almost like real love, and she'd take it. Oh, yes, she would. His strong arms were around her, warm, holding her so tightly.

"C'mon," he said, taking her hand and leading her across the hallway.

Chapter Fifteen

Adam tugged her across the hallway to her bed and threw back the covers.

Stacy climbed in and pulled the covers up to her neck. "I...just want you to hold me for a while until I fall asleep."

"I can do that," he said. "I'll do anything you want."

Her hopes plummeted. Great. Now *this* had become another grand gesture on his part. A favor. Yes, she got it. He would do anything for her, the *mother* of his baby. But as he stood shirtless, wearing only the dark slacks he'd married her in, he slid her a slow smile.

"Whatever you want. Whenever. You just say the

word." His smile turned less tender and far more wolfish.

Oh, oh! A sharp spike of desire sliced through her and she smiled back.

"Just the holding for now, please."

"As you wish."

He unceremoniously dove to the other side of the bed, on top of the covers, stretching out his long legs. In two seconds, he'd moved close enough to pull her into his arms flush against him, her back to his front. His chin rested in the dip between her neck and shoulder.

"Is this okay?"

"Y-yes," she said, trembling a little. It had been so long since she'd spooned like this with anyone.

He was on top of the covers and she was under them. Close, but apart, with a barrier between them. Good metaphor for their relationship, but also about all she could handle tonight. The one and only time she'd been with Adam, she'd been in the best physical shape of her life. Grace had talked her into a yoga class and in a weak moment, Stacy caved. True, they'd both spent far too much time butt-in-chair, their hands on a keyboard. She'd needed the exercise. Though Stacy had never been overweight, she was tall and big-boned. Those few months of yoga tightened and sculpted every muscle in her body. *That* was the woman Adam had taken to bed.

Now, she was fleshy and soft. Plump but healthy. Still, she didn't even recognize her own body. She loathed to admit to her own insecurities, but were Adam to see her naked, whatever desire he'd felt for her might evaporate. A man truly in love with a woman would be able to overlook those bodily imperfections in his wife or lover, but their relationship had been purely physical. Almost primal from the start.

No wonder she had a hang-up.

"Um, Adam?" She waited a beat. "Thank you for marrying me."

"You're welcome. Thank you for marrying *me*."

"But I am sorry that you had to."

"Wrong. I didn't have to do anything. I *had the honor* of marrying you." He whispered the words into the nape of her neck.

"You don't have to say that."

"I know I don't."

"Jeez. Did anyone ever tell you that you're perfect?"

He snorted. "Not at all. Far from it, actually. I can be jealous, selfish, unreasonable and...cruel."

"Not you."

"Yes," he said, his voice sounding quiet, pained.

It made her wonder again what lay underneath his perfect exterior. He was obviously hurting. Damaged. But not great talking about his feelings. If she wanted to help him, she couldn't continue to *guess* what hurt. She assumed a combination of grief and PTSD from his missions.

Suddenly his arms tightened around her. "Plus, I obviously can't put up tree lights worth a damn."

She laughed at that, causing her to move, and accidently press against a very hard part of his anatomy. She froze, supremely grateful to be turned away from him so he couldn't witness her huge smile.

"Sorry about that," he said with a deep chuckle. "But I'm not a machine."

A thrum of exhilaration spiked through her. Adam was quite obviously attracted to her. She wasn't just the saintly mother of his baby. Someone to put on a pedestal, respect and revere, and nothing more. She could still turn him on in the most basic of ways. All hope was *not* lost. Maybe she *was* a little bit the sex-goddess bride after all.

"Actually, it's good to know that I can still do that kind of thing to a man." She rolled to face him. "So, thank you."

"Stacy, you have *got* to be kidding me. You're beautiful, and so damn sexy that I struggle every day to keep my hands off of you." His warm hand slid down her arm and settled on her hip.

The move felt quite different from all the other times he touched her casually and affectionately. She felt branded by the heat of those hands on her body.

"That's nice of you to say, but I don't look the same anymore underneath my clothes. I'm not the woman you slept with all those months ago."

"Would you like a second opinion?" His grin was positively boyish.

The idea was intriguing, but at this point, sex would have to be on her terms. "It would have to be in the dark."

He frowned. "That's a deal breaker. I'm going to need to see every inch of you."

"Not happening, bub." She tousled his hair.

"Why not? You weren't shy with me before."

Their faces were so close, just mere inches from each other. His hand continued to circle her hip in smooth, slow movements.

Eager to touch him, she palmed his chin. "I think…that night, I might have been a little bit out of my mind."

"We both were."

"I know it's crazy, but right from the beginning, I thought we would be more. I didn't want just the one night."

"Neither did I." He took her hand and brushed a kiss across her knuckles. "It just worked out that way."

"And yet here we are. *Married*."

"Here we are." Adam pressed his forehead to hers.

"Adam, you know that you can tell me anything, right? And I won't judge you."

"Okay. I believe you. It's just that I like to keep the past where it belongs."

She refrained from telling him that the past wasn't *where* it belonged when it continued to haunt him. For a moment, she didn't say anything, just studied his heated gaze.

"Tonight, you saw that my mother was very upset with me, and you should know why. She suggested that I go back to Chicago with her and go to the VA there. She reminded me that servicemen are often separated from their wives and I can get medical care anywhere."

He reached for her hand and threaded their fingers together. "I know she's not my biggest fan, but she has to know that's never an ideal situation."

"You have to understand my mother. When I left Chicago, it was at least in part to put some distance between us. I'm an only child, and she's had a difficult time letting me go. Sometimes…it's not healthy."

He nodded. "Have you decided what you're going to do?"

"I'm not going back. Not until sometime after our baby is born, anyway. I'll revisit at that time, but for now I'm going to stay here in Charming with you."

"Thank you, Stacy." His warm dark eyes were shimmering.

She reached behind her to turn off the lamp. "No, thank *you*. For making this decision so easy. You're a good man and I'm so lucky that you're going to be my child's father. It was the best decision I never made."

"You and me both." Adam chuckled. "Now go to sleep before I kiss you and turn on every light in the house."

The idea was titillating, and a wave of awareness rolled through her. How well she remembered those warm lips claiming hers. The feel of his strong body pressed against hers.

"I don't think I can sleep."

"Try. You look tired."

Stacy murmured her agreement and closed her eyes. One hand on Adam's chest, she both listened and felt the pattern of his breathing shift and slow.

Stacy opened her eyes and blinked to adjust her vision. The room had darkened, as only ambient moonlight filtered through the blinds. She went up on one elbow to find Adam no longer lying next to her. Disappointing, sure, but she'd only asked him to stay until she fell asleep. She heard a rustling near the window and turned toward the sound.

Adam stood, his back to her, head bent. He straightened and ran a hand through his hair. Frustration seemed to pour out of him, written in his rigid pose, his tense shoulders.

She wondered if he'd had a nightmare and she hadn't heard him thrashing around. Sometimes a wave of sadness would pass over him and Stacy could almost physically see him willing it away for her sake. So that he could keep up the role of wonderful and supportive father to be. But it couldn't go on much longer before he'd break. She wished he'd open up and allow back some of the support he'd given her. But he was far too much of a gentleman to admit that he still missed his first wife. He must have loved her so much.

Okay, stop comparing. You're pathetic. You can't seriously be jealous of Mandy.

No, of course not. But maybe she was simply envious of being with Adam at a time before he'd been emotionally wounded. Distant. Maybe no longer able to love someone as completely as he had his first wife.

Undaunted, she threw off the covers and slipped out of bed. She wanted to touch him, to bring him back. He tipped his head slightly as he heard her behind him. This time she touched him first, wrapping her arms around his waist, pressing her lips and tongue against the coolness of his taut back. The night, the dark, gave her courage to be bold. He made a deep male sound of appreciation and turned to face her. Without preamble or tenderness, his lips crashed down on hers, taking her without question. With total authority. His mouth ravaged hers, his tongue firm and plundering.

He broke the kiss on a ragged breath. "Tell me to stop."

"Don't you dare."

"God, what you do to me, baby." His hands were under her gown, easily bringing it up and over her head in one swift motion.

Hands firm on her behind, he carried her back to the bed. She went up on her knees, and between the two of them, they divested him of his pants and underwear quickly.

She tumbled back on the pillow and Adam braced

himself above her, his strong and sinewy arms pinning her in place.

"I remember this," he said on a ragged breath.

"So do I." And it felt like everything inside her that mattered was waking up again.

Once, she'd had hot sex with a stranger. Only he'd never felt like a stranger somehow. But now, she knew a lot more about Adam. Even if she didn't know everything, all that she knew and understood drew her even closer to him. This was real intimacy, this stripping of the layers of emotion right along with the clothes. He felt like her soul mate, like someone from whom she'd been accidentally separated through no fault of their own.

"The most erotic night of my life." Adam met her gaze, unflinching.

His dark irises were warm, and okay, she had to say it: delicious.

The most erotic night of his *life*. All right. She'd take it.

Stacy spread her legs and wound her hands around his neck. He kissed her, long and warm and deep, with the taste of sweet tea on his tongue. Adam could kiss her all night long and she could be satisfied with only that. He made kissing a sporting event. No, an Olympic event, where he'd take the gold. And the silver. Oh, gosh, and the bronze, too.

His open-mouthed kisses slid down the column of her neck, and he kissed along her cool bare skin, leaving trails of his heat behind. He lingered at her breasts, then lower, stopping only briefly on her belly. He kissed her thighs, her knees, even her feet.

"Adam," she moaned, reaching for him, pulling him up to her by his shoulders.

Reaching to stroke him, she finally got his attention. Eyes as hot as molten lava pierced her, letting her see how much she'd affected him, how much he wanted her.

"Please. Get inside me," she whispered. "Now."

She didn't have to wait for long. Adam thrust inside her, making them both moan. They moved together, in a perfect rhythm, their bodies in sync with each other. His even, powerful pumps stoked a raging fire inside her. She'd once wondered if that first time could have been a fluke. Maybe she'd been lonely, and alone for so long that just one touch from a good-looking man had her go off.

But *this* was proof positive their magic hadn't been a one-time thing. This moment was all Adam, making her body thrum and ache, and long for release. She finally did, an orgasm rolling through her, making her entire body pulse, and hum, and tremble. Adam followed her, his own release giving her another wave of intense pleasure she'd have never thought possible.

They were both still breathing hard when he tugged her into his arms. She buried her face in his warm neck, trying to catch her breath.

"Unbelievable," Adam said, holding her tightly,

pressing a kiss to her temple. "And I didn't think it could get any better."

"So it's not just me. That was...incredible."

"Hot. We're good together. So good."

"Hmm. Adam? Let's just enjoy this, okay?"

"What do you mean?"

"Let's enjoy being together, like this, and not ask for anything more from each other. *This* is enough for me."

"Stacy," he said in a low, hushed, almost warning tone.

"No, I mean it. You and I have something powerful and rare, more than some married couples ever have. We like each other, we're having a baby and we love having sex."

If love was missing from the equation, she was okay with that. Love, and being too attached to an outcome, screwed everything up. High expectations ruined a couple.

He rolled away from her, and braced himself above her, so she could see his eyes. They were the same sad eyes she couldn't forget. But now they were filled with a new emotion, one she couldn't easily decipher.

"Look at me. I'm never going to shortchange you. You're going to have every part of me, not just my body. I'm your husband."

"I know, but, baby, sometimes a piece of paper is exactly what it sounds like. People who love each other don't need it, and for those that don't love each other, it does nothing at all."

"You don't need to love me, Stacy. Whatever you can give me is enough."

She smoothed his cheek with the back of her hand. "It's enough for me, too. But I need your full attention. Don't let your mind take you somewhere I can't go."

He frowned. "When have I done that?"

She thought he'd been more self-aware, but maybe that was part of the problem. "Sometimes you get a dazed look in your eyes and you're...gone. In another place."

"I'm sorry."

"Don't be. But that's why I said you can tell me anything. You can talk to me. About anything."

"I'll snap out of it, don't worry. I'm here for you, I promise you."

"Is it something in the past you regret?" Right here, literally bared to each other, might be a good time for the truth.

His arms tightened around her, but he didn't speak.

"There's something I didn't tell you." Maybe if she started, if she shared her mistakes. "That last relationship I was in? I lived with a man who had been divorced for years, and I thought he loved me. But I caught him cheating on me, with his ex-wife."

"What?"

"You heard me. Those two idiots never got out of each other's systems. Don't get me wrong, it was unhealthy. They were dysfunctional and they brought me into their mess. It seems like all I've ever been part of is unhealthy relationships."

"Stacy—"

She put a finger to his lips. "Let me finish. They got back together after we broke up and remarried. That's why I mentioned that a piece of paper doesn't do anything to love. Divorce couldn't stop them from continuing to love each other."

"That's...ridiculous."

"Yeah, I guess." Stacy chuckled. "Obsessive love. Not healthy at all. I wish they hadn't involved me in their dysfunction."

"I hate that happened to you. Hate it." He drew her hand to his lips, kissed it. "None of it was your fault, I hope you know."

"I do now, but it took a while getting there. Too many times we blame ourselves for something we couldn't have stopped even if we *wanted* to. It wasn't my fault." She allowed that statement to settle between them.

"I'm not ready to talk about it yet," Adam said, gently rubbing her back. "Okay?"

"Yeah," she said. "I don't mind going first. I just bared myself to you, completely."

"Nice try." He rolled to face her. "I still haven't seen you naked with every light in the house on."

"So you're going to play hardball."

"Oh, yes I am, babe. Yes, I am."

Chapter Sixteen

When Stacy woke the next morning, Adam's warm hand rested on her belly. She could feel his slow even breaths as he slept on his stomach beside her. This was exactly what she'd missed: the morning after. She was getting everything she'd wanted—Adam sleeping peacefully beside her. They were just as explosive together as she'd remembered. And now, she was his wife.

His *wife*.

That meant he was her husband. She had a *husband*. The word rolled in her brain as she tried to accept her new reality. So many huge changes had happened lately. They were all welcome, but all took getting used to, and she'd just become accustomed to being Adam's roommate. Now she was his wife, and...lover? She hoped. This could be the start of something between them, something real. She made a promise to herself that she wouldn't ask for too much from him, too soon.

It was enough that he wanted her physically, too. And that could grow into love someday. Love, and companionship, and respect. It was up to her not to feel like a second choice, because Adam belonged to her now. And she could be his, too, in every way.

"Adam?" she said softly, turning her body toward him.

His hand slipped off her stomach and he groaned, opening one eye. "Hey."

"Hi. You know what I was thinking just now?" She tweaked his chin.

"That we should do this all over again?"

"Well, no, but...okay, that would be good, too. But you should stop sleeping in that other bedroom. This is your bed and I want to share it with you."

"Yeah?" He gave her a sleepy smile. "If that's what you want, you got it."

Oh, damn, this was getting annoying. "No, Adam. I want this only if *you* want it, too. Stop making me feel like you'll do or say anything to make me happy."

He quirked an eyebrow but didn't say a word.

Even as she'd said the words out loud, she heard the ridiculousness of them. But, well...she wanted to dig deeper into Adam and really *know* him. Reveal what he kept hidden from her because maybe it wasn't too pleasant. She needed all of him for this to work at all.

"I mean…what I meant to say is, this is a two-way street. Okay? Do you want to sleep with me, or not?"

His hand dove under the covers, exploring, and tweaked her nipple. "I have to be honest. I don't care if there's any actual sleeping involved."

And then he rolled on top of her and made love to her all over again.

After Adam left for work later that morning for the afternoon shift, Stacy took a shower.

Everything had changed. She and Adam were back to a type of intimacy, and at least they had that. But she still didn't know how she would crack the mystery that was Adam Cruz. Here was a man who'd seen some of the worst things a human could see, who'd lost someone important to him, and yet he refused to talk about any of it.

For now, all she wanted was to help him heal enough to be a good father to their child.

After drying off and dressing, Stacy checked her email. Her editor notes had arrived, and with them the green light to move forward with this book. Stacy had a tight deadline now, with little time built in for further edits down the road. She settled in at the kitchen counter and went right to work, excited about this project, the energy of creativity buzzing and zapping all around her. Even so, every few minutes her ring finger caught her attention. The glittering, matching gold band she wore now. It was both a pleasure and an out-of-body experience every time she caught the glint of gold and remembered. It would take some getting used to, this marriage thing.

A few hours later, she'd written two chapters, a record. She took a break, stretched her legs and made next month's appointment with the ob-gyn at the VA in Houston. By then Adam should have all the paperwork through and addition of her as cobeneficiary. At her last appointment in Montana, everything had been progressing normally, so she wasn't at all worried.

Her phone buzzed, and she picked it up to read a text from Adam telling her that he'd made her a sandwich before he left, but that he'd be just as happy to have lunch delivered to her. She texted back that she'd have the sandwich, but truthfully all she wanted to do was read. This always happened when it was time for her to write a book. She gazed longingly at the stack of reading on the table and wondered if she should make another trip to Once Upon a Book. After all, Mr. Finch said they needed the business. Lord knew she often single-handedly supported local bookstores.

But no, she had enough books. She hadn't even finished reading these. Then again...

Stacy wondered how her mother was doing, and whether she should apologize. Maybe just to smooth over the tension between them. *Somebody* had to be the bigger person. She wanted for her little girl to have two grandmothers in her life, and quite frankly, she'd feel a lot better asking her own mother about breastfeeding and the nitty-gritty of postpartum. None of it, other than the baby, sounded like a whole lot of fun.

But instead of calling her mother, Stacy stuffed her face with the sandwich Adam made for her.

After eating, she phoned Grace.

"I hate you," she answered. "It's twenty degrees today. Twenty!"

"I'm sorry." She hesitated to tell Grace that the weather forecast was for the temperature to drop to the sixties today, a cooling trend. "You'll have to come visit again soon."

"What's up? How was the honeymoon? Was it too awful?"

"Um…"

Then, Stacy told everything. Well, almost everything. And even then, she raised a hand to her warm cheek just remembering. The man was a fantastic lover.

"See, I told you I wasn't imagining those looks he gave you. He has the hots for you still."

"Apparently."

"So…" Grace prompted. "And what else?"

"Nothing else. Not for now." She refused to discuss sex with Grace. It might wind up in one of her books. "Did you talk to my mother?"

"Yes. She explained this is what you do. Get your

hopes up on a man and he always lets you down.
Blah, blah, blah. She's such a *complete downer* it's
no wonder you turned out the way you did."

Stacy scoffed. "Oh, yeah? And how did I *turn
out*?"

"You write thrillers. Maybe you're a little jaded
about love?"

"I'll have you know I've dated plenty. What about
Daniel? We had something for a while."

And in those first years, what they'd had together
seemed real. They didn't play games with each other.
Honesty went a long way. Well, she'd thought so until
she opened door number three: Dominique, never
quite out of his system.

"I never met Daniel, but he sounds like a real
chump. Who goes back with the ex-wife he complained about constantly?"

"Someone desperately in love with her?"

"Honey, that isn't love. Obsession is *not* love, don't
kid yourself."

"Maybe." But Stacy wanted to believe that she'd
recognize love when she saw it.

Then again, when she tried to remember examples
of healthy love, she couldn't think of any. Her relationships had almost always been lopsided. Either
a guy was too crazy about her, and she was luke-
warm, or she was the one crazy about the guy. And
he was…well, he was Daniel.

And now, Adam. While it felt like she'd entered
lopsided territory again, this did seem different.

Adam was the exception. She didn't have to fall in love with Adam or need him to fall for her. The fact was they were now inextricably bound together by one random event. But he still wasn't letting her inside that mind and heart of his. And without their baby, she wasn't sure they had anything in common other than a mutual enjoyment of each other's bodies. While she realized this was far more than many married couples had, in order to make it through this year she wanted to fully know Adam. Understand his psyche, because she'd already been with a man who hid things from her.

"So, um, did my mother say anything else?"

"Nothing you want to hear."

"She didn't even tell me when she's going back to Chicago."

"She doesn't have a flight yet. Her plan was to wait to fly back with you, I guess. So she's probably going to be looking at flights today or tomorrow."

Great. More guilt piled on Stacy. Her mother was sitting in a hotel room in Houston, probably hating her life. Waiting for Stacy to call and apologize. Well, she'd be waiting for a while because Stacy had nothing to apologize for.

Her story didn't have to be her mother's story. Maybe Grace really had rubbed off on Stacy, because she refused to paint all men with one broad brush. And Adam had already proven himself to be an anomaly.

The doorbell rang and that hadn't happened since

she'd moved in, so she wondered if it could be the UPS guy. She'd started shopping for baby clothes, and they would be arriving soon.

"I've got to go, Grace. There's someone at the door."

It wasn't the UPS guy, but Susannah from next door. She held a tray of cookies in front of her.

"Ava and I used to have a routine some mornings," she explained. "She'd bring her coffee beans over, grind them and make me the most delicious coffee in existence. I provided the pastries."

"Please come in," Stacy said, eyeing a cookie with pink piped icing. "Adam isn't here."

"I know, sugar. I saw him leave earlier. He waved to me, big smile, just as happy as he could be."

Hmm. She rather hoped last night had put a spring in his step. It certainly had for her. Stacy led her to the kitchen counter, where Susannah set the tray of cookies.

"Milk?" Stacy asked. "I gave up coffee. There's no point without the caffeine."

"That's a great idea. Lots of calcium for the baby." Susannah shooed Stacy to sit. "Let me do it, child."

Reminding herself that her neighbor was simply being kind, and that didn't mean she believed Stacy was helpless, she sat. "Everyone's always waiting on me and it isn't necessary."

"Enjoy it while you can." She set down a couple of glasses. "I actually wanted to talk to you while Adam isn't here."

"What about?" Stacy reached for the pink iced cookie and took a bite. It tasted as delicious as it looked—silky sweet sugar, with a hint of coconut.

"I know who you are."

Stacy froze in midbite. "Wh-what do you mean?"

"The writer. Piper Lawrence. That's you, isn't it?" She sat beside Stacy and reached for a cookie in the shape of a reindeer.

"Um, I..." Well, the jig was up. *"Who told you?"*

"No one. I read your book."

"Oh." Stacy slid down in her chair. "Well, I'm very sorry about that."

"Sorry? Why sorry? At first, I wasn't sure it could be you. So I went to my bookshelf and found my dog-eared book. Sorry about the dog ears, by the way. That's you, in the back of the book. With a lot of makeup."

So much for airbrushed Piper looking nothing like Stacy. Apparently, there was at least a passing resemblance. "I asked Adam not to tell anyone."

"He *knows*?" Susannah sat back, eyes wide.

Stacy nodded and could almost hear the unsaid words: *and he married you, anyway?*

"Of course, he does."

"And here I was worried it was your big secret. Mr. Finch said that you came into the bookstore, but you didn't say a word to him."

"He knows, too?" Stacy dropped her cookie.

"He recognized you right away and when you left went to find your book to confirm his suspicions."

"Oh, great. Just great."

"I can understand why you want some anonymity, but, honey, you have to know how we love a writer! You *do* know about our poetry club, don't you?"

"Sure, of course."

"That's right, Patsy dedicated one of her poems to you, as a wedding gift. Well, we weren't sure you were going to stay in Charming, but now that it appears you are…we'd love you to become an honorary member of the Almost Dead Poet Society!"

"Me?" Stacy squeaked.

"It would be such an honor to have a bona fide author among us. You'll be our in-house writer. Of course, you're not a senior citizen, but we'll relax the rules. We love the young people who attend, but none of them are official members. You would be the first."

"But I'm really not that…"

"Good?"

"Um, well, I was going to say famous. No one knows me outside of my editor, my agent and my readers." And then Stacy confessed the honest-to-God truth. "I just like to be anonymous."

"We won't tell anyone else, we promise!" Susannah held up her palm as if to swear on a bible.

"It's not that I'm hiding it, exactly, but well… I really don't want people wondering where I get my ideas."

"Very understandable, sugar. That bathroom scene? I didn't sleep for *weeks*."

"See, that doesn't help."

"If that's all you're worried about, you should know that Mr. Finch and I are the only ones who've actually *read* your book. Everyone else prefers historical fiction, and, of course, romance."

"Well, thank goodness for that."

"We'd like to do more outreach. Next week, our first reading at the bookstore for the kids. We're all going to take turns reading a childhood favorite. I thought you'd be perfect because you're a professional author *and* a mother-to-be. What could be better?"

"Okay, well, sure. I want to help, of course."

Stacy had participated in enough of her own private book readings to know what she was doing. It would give her something to do during these long months that lay ahead. She helped herself to another cookie, this one a black-and-white.

"And if you have any questions about motherhood, or anything at all, feel free to ask." Susannah patted Stacy's leg. "I know everything you'll ever need to know is on the World Wide Web. But I raised four children, so I have a few tricks, and I know you're far from your mother right now."

At the words, Stacy felt unexpected tears sting her eyes. She'd written and read about "found family" but she honestly never thought that would be her.

"Thank you. That's kind and I might take you up on it."

"Do you have a crib yet?"

In Chicago, her mother had already purchased a crib, without Stacy's input. At the time, she'd simply been grateful for one less item on her long to-do checklist. The room was also decorated pink, even though Stacy hadn't had a gender reveal. She swallowed back more tears at the thought that she'd taken all this from her mother. The chance to live with her daughter and granddaughter and relive those happy years they'd all spent together: the three musketeers.

"No crib, but I'll start shopping for one pretty soon."

"Let me help." Susannah stood. "Let's go shopping!"

Chapter Seventeen

Several minutes later, Stacy, Susannah and her little poodle, Doodle, were in her Cadillac Oldsmobile, pulling over on another residential street.

"We just have to pick up Roy," Susannah said.

"Mr. Finch? He's coming, too?"

"Yes, and Lois. Unfortunately, Etta Mae and Patsy can't make it." Susannah parked near the driveway of a small cottage house with blue-and-gray siding. "It might be too much walking for Patsy."

"I don't understand. Why are we *all* going?"

"Oh, sugar, we don't get out much. This is an *event*." She unlocked the passenger-side door as Mr. Finch approached. "Did I not mention that we're all pooling our money together to buy you this crib?"

"What? Oh, no, I can't let *you* pay for this!"

"This is a gift from the Almost Dead Poet Society. We started paying dues last year, thinking that we were going to give a donation to a literacy program, but then you came along. You're going to be our in-house writer and honorary member."

Oh, boy. Stacy didn't remember having agreed to that yet. "Um, well…"

Mr. Finch opened the door and eased his long legs into the back seat. "Heavens, are we bringing *Doodle* along to get a crib?"

Doodle began prancing and turning like he'd been reunited with his best friend, then settled himself in Mr. Finch's lap.

"I've got his leash. He'll wait outside while we shop," Susannah said. "I can't leave him alone for too long. He has an anxiety attack."

One more stop, and Lois piled in, sweetly kissing Mr. Finch on the lips. "Hello, darling."

"Hi, baby," Mr. Finch drawled in his deep Texas accent.

Love was in the air, senior-citizen style. She'd heard recently that Lois and Mr. Finch had both been married before, and quite happily. It was sweet, the thought that one might have two great loves of their lives.

"Off we go to buy a crib!" Susannah announced, and drove off.

Once they'd arrived and started walking the rows of samples, Stacy didn't think that picking the right crib would ever be this complicated. Of course, she knew what she wanted safety-wise. But she hadn't expected the white princess canopy crib. It was beautiful, perfect for a sweet girlie girl.

Which she didn't know for certain that she'd be having. That initial instinct had begun to dull a little more every day.

"I like this brown." Lois touched the rail of a cherrywood canopy crib. "It's warm and welcoming."

Mr. Finch whipped out his tape measure again, as he'd been doing for every single crib in the entire store. After the second attempt, Stacy gave up explaining that every crib was now made according to the new safety standards. Instead, he seemed to think they were still constructing rails with three-inch-wide death traps.

"Yep, passes standards."

"What would we do without you, Roy?" Lois said, rubbing his back.

He smiled so widely that Stacy understood whom he was actually trying to impress. A curl of delight went through her and she briefly wondered why her mother had never even *tried* to find love again.

"Whatever you'd like, dear." Mr. Finch spread his hands wide, encompassing the store. "This is our gift to you."

Eventually, Stacy did decide on the cherrywood crib Lois admired because she was correct. It gave off a sense of warmth and home, just what she wanted for her newborn, boy or girl. She'd been forced to admit that nothing but her own hopes had been responsible for her "intuition" that she might be having a daughter. It might be Adam's influence, and either the fleeting thought, or fervent hope, she might have a boy who looked like his father.

On the ride back, the senior citizens all chatted about their upcoming book reading at Once Upon a Book. The owner had started advertising and there was considerable interest in the event. Mr. Finch would be reading *Where the Wild Things Are,* and Lois had chosen *Black Beauty.*

"What would you like to read, dear?" Susannah glanced at Stacy.

"I don't know if I should find out whether I'm having a boy or a girl," Stacy blurted out, wildly off-topic. "I could find out at the next ultrasound."

Conversation ceased. Doodle, now seated on Stacy's lap, gave her a doe-eyed look. She then turned twice and settled down for a nap.

"What does Adam say?" Mr. Finch asked.

"I haven't asked him."

"I'm sure he doesn't care one way or the other," Susannah said. "He's a smart man."

"Do you have a feeling one way or another?" Lois asked. "I always knew, and I was right every time."

"You had a fifty-fifty chance," Mr. Finch said.

Susannah smiled at their friendly exchange, as if she was used to these two. They bantered back and forth, in a friendly way, all the way back to the house. Susannah pulled into her driveway.

The issue then became who would carry the large box inside the house that an attendant had helped them load.

"I can do it," Mr. Finch said. "I just need a dolly."

"Don't be silly! Your back," Lois said.

"You know what? I bet I can do this." Stacy rubbed her hands together.

From the horrified expressions on their faces, all three firmly disagreed.

Stacy went hands on hips. "I'm serious. It makes a lot more sense than either one of you hurting yourself. Really, if it's too heavy I'll give up."

"Or we could wait for Adam," Lois said, pulling on Mr. Finch's arm.

Then, all three shook their heads, crossed their arms and blocked the trunk of Susannah's car.

Adam found a strange sight next door when he parked in the driveway of his home. Susannah and some of the other members of the Almost Dead Poet Society were blocking Stacy from the trunk of the Cadillac Olds next door. Interesting. Never a dull moment around these seniors.

They seemed to be in some kind of a standoff. Stacy, arms crossed. Seniors, three of them, arms crossed. Clearly, she was outnumbered.

"Adam! How wonderful. Our troubles are over." Susannah tossed up her hands.

Stacy's arms remained solidly in place, but she did

give him a once-over, curiosity in her eyes. "You're home early."

"We prevented a near disaster," Lois said.

"Your wife insisted on trying to haul the new crib inside on her own." Mr. Finch shook his head as if this was a preposterous idea.

"A crib? We have a crib?" He turned to Stacy.

"I've tried to explain that they were already kind enough to *buy* it for us, and then they'd rather hurt themselves than let *me* bring it in." Stacy finally un-crossed her arms.

"Y'all bought us a *crib*?"

He probably sounded like a stuck record. He and Stacy had talked in passing about a crib, but at the time he wasn't sure where that crib would be located. And, damn, this made it all so very real. There was going to be a baby, who would need a place to sleep. A real baby, not just one that existed in his imagination.

He was going to be a father. It seemed he was still getting used to the idea.

"It's our gift to you!" Susannah said. "Our group had some money saved up and it couldn't go to a more deserving couple. And Stacy, our honorary member, and in-house poet."

"Wait a minute now." Stacy pointed. "You said in-house *writer*. I can't write poetry to save my life!"

"Well, now, sugar, everybody says that at first." Lois waved dismissively.

"Look at me." Roy spread his arms. "I'd never done anything remotely like this."

"Now, his poems about Texas are Valerie's favorites," Susannah said.

"But—"

Before this conversation spiraled further downhill, Adam put a stop to it. "All right, let me at this crib."

The seniors parted to let him through, and Susannah popped open the trunk. He hauled out the box and carried it inside the house, everyone following.

"We should get going, ladies," Roy said at the door. "Let these two decide where to put the crib and set it up. Adam, should you need any help putting it together, give me a call."

"Thanks, Roy. I've got this." He propped the box against the wall. "Y'all come by the Salty Dog soon and lunch is my treat."

"Stacy, I'll be in touch soon about your honorary membership." Susannah waved and went back to her car with the others.

Adam shut the door and turned to Stacy. "What's this honorary membership thing?"

Stacy covered her face. "I've been outed. They know I'm a writer, and now I've not only been asked to be an honorary member, but I've been invited to join them and read at the bookstore during children's story time."

"From *your* book?" Sue him, he was new to this parenting gig, but this didn't sound like a good idea.

"No, silly." She swatted his arm. "From my favorite children's book."

"Nothing wrong with that. Right?"

"No, that's fine. I don't mind the reading. But… I'm not a poet."

He shrugged. "Then don't do it."

"Are you crazy? I can't refuse them! They're so… *nice*."

"Aw, Stacy." He pulled her into the tight circle of his arms and pressed a kiss to her temple. "You're sweeter than you want anyone to know."

"Keep that to yourself, mister." She drilled a finger into his chest.

Damn, he'd missed her today so much that when there was a lull this afternoon, he'd knocked off early, leaving Brian in charge. Last night had been… incredible. Just like the first time, when he'd been out of his mind with lust. He honestly hadn't expected sex to be anywhere near as good as the first time. It was too high a bar.

There had to have been something different and special about that night. Maybe it was the song, "Tennessee Whiskey." Or the fact he hadn't talked with a woman candidly for years. Maybe the fact he hadn't been with anyone else in a long while. That he hadn't *wanted* anyone else.

Not until Stacy.

She'd breezed into his life one night and he'd honestly never been the same. It hadn't been just that one crazy night, but the two of them together. They were explosive.

Now, he wanted to get her both naked and happy,

but also show her he could put this crib together. He could demonstrate his usefulness to her outside of the bedroom. So he settled for something in between, giving her a soul-deep kiss, which she returned.

When they came up for air, he tweaked her nose. "I haven't forgotten that it was dark when I got you naked. I'm still holding out for some natural light."

"Don't hold your breath."

"I'll be patient." He let go of her and headed to the box with singular purpose. "Where do you want this? Still in the...bedroom?"

He hesitated because so far it had been "her bedroom" and "his bedroom." And while she'd already invited him into her bed, that was last night, in the afterglow. He didn't want to be presumptuous.

"In our bedroom?" She walked ahead of him down the hallway, then stopped and turned. "Or... we do have a spare room. Maybe in here?"

She'd pointed toward the bedroom where he'd been staying. It was directly across the hall so she wouldn't be far from the baby. And it just dawned on him that this crib had a larger meaning attached to it.

"Sure, that's perfect."

And now more than anything, he wanted this crib up so it could be an anchor.

The idea was ridiculous because he knew better than most how quickly the items in a small house could be packed up. How swiftly and thoroughly a life could change in an instant. He understood things, and people, could be gone in a flash. For the last few years, he'd had little tying him to any one place. This now, with her, would be different. He could sense it in the air all around him and could see it in her eyes.

She wasn't going to leave him.

She'd gone into the smaller bedroom, where he found her moving his sleeping bag, pillow and a few other things to the wall that faced the window.

"Right here would be good."

"Great." He heaved the box inside and used the pocketknife he always carried with him to slice open the box.

"Hmm. It looked so different in the store."

He turned to find her smiling. "Now who's a wiseass?"

Crouching on his haunches, he surveyed the parts. "I'm going to need a screwdriver, possibly a hammer and a PhD in engineering."

And an hour later, Adam fervently wished he had that degree as Stacy sat cross-legged on the floor reading the instructions out loud. He didn't understand how a Navy SEAL who'd planned and deployed complicated missions could be so thwarted by a simple crib. It made him wonder and fear what fatherhood would be like. He'd hardly gotten used to the idea, but the reality would likely be far different.

This baby, a human life, would be completely and totally dependent on him for protection. And what if he had a son instead of the daughter that Stacy believed she was going to have? He might have someone *like him*. The thought filled him with apprehension, because at eight, he'd climbed a tree, believing he could fly. It was his sister, talking him into waiting for his parents so they could take a photo of him flying, who saved him from a broken leg. Or worse.

And he sure hoped that Stacy knew more about babies than he did. It would be a mistake to simply assume, so he should probably investigate soon. Otherwise, they'd be in this together, with neither one of them having any idea what they were doing. Far away from the grandparents.

Jesus, was it hot in this room?

"I think that goes right here." Stacy pointed to a nut, pulling him out of his daze.

"No, it goes here." He adjusted the nut in place.

"Oh, that's right." She laid the directions on the floor beside him and stood with a sigh. "I'll be right back."

"Go ahead, do what you have to do. I've got this."

He picked up the paper, examining the layout, and tried to understand why the picture didn't match reality.

Nope. He didn't have this.

Chapter Eighteen

Stacy had to leave the room or risk laughing out loud. She'd never seen Adam look more adorable, this tall man on the floor trying to put together a crib. Endearing, and rumpled, and sexy, making it difficult not to pull him away from this task and straight into their bedroom. *Their bedroom.* But Adam would want to see her, all of her, and she didn't know if she was ready for that.

After crossing the hallway, Stacy shut the door to the bedroom. Poised in front of the mirror over the dresser, she viewed a woman whose body had changed and would continue to change. She could decide this was a process she would endure, or one she would celebrate. And she wanted to be pleased with her changing body because carrying a child should be a joyous time.

Slowly, she peeled off her clothes in front of the mirror because she hadn't really taken a good hard look at herself in over a month. Her breasts were larger, the nipples rosy and tight. She turned to the side to examine her swollen belly. Her skin was stretching, but there were no stretch marks and her skin felt silky and supple as her fingers slid across her stomach.

Dare she say it? Her skin *glowed* with an almost pinkish hue.

She was *beautiful*. Adam had done this to her. He'd changed her. He'd changed her life, too, and somehow, she'd managed to change his. She'd pulled him out of his fog of grief, and she and the baby would both keep him from going back to that dark place. All she had to do was be patient, and one day he'd fully be hers.

Feeling bold, she opened the door and walked out of the bedroom fully naked. She didn't care that the hall light was on, and it was still light outside. Thankfully, though, the shades were drawn because this wasn't a moment she wanted to share with Susannah or any other neighbors. She stood in the doorway, watching Adam as he worked, his back to her. The crib was nearly put together, but more pressing matters were on her mind.

She positioned herself with one hand on her hip, the other braced on the door frame. She then shook her hair and arranged it to fall forward a little, covering the tips of her breasts, giving her a Lady Godiva look. Jutting out a hip, she then worried that the pose looked too ridiculous, while she wanted sexy. And should she pucker her lips, or would she get that sad-duck-face look if she did? Well, damn, she was getting cold now. Her nipples were hard and not because she was turned on. She considered going back for a robe.

"Stacy! Do you realize we need a mattress for this? It didn't come with…" He turned, holding one side of the crib, which he promptly dropped, along with his jaw.

The shock was not exactly what she'd hoped for, and Stacy reached for and shut off the hall light. He could still see her in the light of the room, but at least she didn't feel quite as…exposed.

"The mattress… The mattress was on b-back order. It's being shipped." She turned to go, but he caught her by the elbow.

"No, wait. Let me see you." His gaze appraised her from top to bottom, the shock quickly evaporating.

Now she could see that his expression landed closer to awe. He flicked the hall light back on. She tried to flip it off, but his hand stayed hers before she could.

"You're so beautiful." The pads of his fingers slid down from her shoulder, down her arm, to her hip.

"I think so, too."

"Good."

"Adam, I know this was an accident…" She covered his hand with her own, right where it was positioned on her hip. "Maybe we would have never wound up together otherwise but I'm happy. I've never been happier."

"*This*…doesn't feel like an accident." His eyes darkened with blazing heat.

It felt like love, the kind that arrives as unexpectedly and swiftly as a rogue wave, mowing over anyone in its path. She'd read books about people like this before, but certainly never believed it could happen to her. Or that this kind of love even happened to actual people. Maybe because she'd been jaded, but she'd never felt like this before.

Adam picked her up in his arms and carried her to bed. He made love to her again, all the sweeter this time because it felt so real.

Before leaving for the bookstore reading, Stacy wrapped her only present for Adam. They'd both agreed not to spend money on each other this year and buy for their baby instead. But Stacy found the perfect present at the Artlandish gallery. At one time, she might not have chosen it, but the gift was entirely appropriate, and she believed with all her heart that Adam had come out of the darkness. He'd truly moved on. With her.

He was engaged with her in conversations about family and future plans. They'd made decisions, like a name for the baby, whether boy or girl. It was harder than she'd have ever thought it would be to agree on a boy's name. She wanted to name a boy Adam, Jr. and he refused. They were still metaphorically slugging that one out, but the girl's name had been easy.

They'd chosen the rather unconventional name of Tennessee, a funny name for a Texan, but hey. In Stacy's mind, her daughter would forever be named after a song. A song signifying the night Stacy met the love of her life.

Not only did Stacy feel like she'd healed Adam's heart for their child, but she'd also fallen deeply in love with him. A love greater than she'd believed possible.

The doorbell rang and Stacy opened it to find Susannah. "Ready to go?"

"Just let me get my bag."

Because Adam was working tonight, Stacy would ride over with Susannah. Unfortunately, she had to leave behind Doodle, who could be heard barking next door.

"We're trying some new anxiety medication, but he'll still be sitting behind the door when I get home." Susannah led the way toward her Oldsmobile. "How's the crib? Is it up yet?"

The crib still wasn't up because she and Adam were spending every spare moment in bed. It was a little ridiculous how attracted she'd become to him. Last night, he'd been taking out the trash and she'd practically jumped him. Quite frankly, sex was a good way to both get and keep his attention.

"Not yet—we thought maybe we'd wait until the mattress arrives."

She turned to Stacy as she started the car and pulled out of the driveway. "There's still plenty of time."

They arrived a few minutes later and walked inside to see the bookstore decorated with children's book themes. There were wall hangings of Beatrix Potter books, Ramona the Pest, Harry Potter and others. Near the entrance, a stack of books in the shape of a Christmas tree was approximately four feet high. Bookmarks hung from between the pages of the books. As she passed, Stacy turned one over and noticed that the bookmark had a child's name written on the back and their wish for a particular book.

"That's the wish tree. It's for the children of lower-income families. We want to encourage them to keep reading." Susannah pointed to the books. "Ava's idea."

Stacy quickly grabbed ten bookmarks. She'd recently received a direct deposit in her checking account from her publisher, and Adam had refused the money she'd tried to give him for groceries, and the water and electric bills. She was flush for now.

Adults browsed for books with their children. Good to know they were getting some business tonight.

The children took seats on the small square rugs

that had been placed in the center of an open area. As the reading began with Mr. Finch and *Where the Wild Things Are*, Stacy stayed off to the side with Ava and Valerie. All the senior citizens took their turn reading. Books like *'Twas the Night Before Christmas, Goodnight Moon* and others. When it was finally Stacy's turn, she sat in the chair of honor, and took in all the happy children's faces. They seemed to range in age from a two-year-old toddler to a school-age kid.

Stacy had chosen *Love You Forever*, the classic story about a mother's lifelong love for her son. She read to the children, and thought that someday, maybe her son or daughter might be listening to her read in this very bookstore if she and Adam stayed in Charming. And what a wonderful place to live, where there were float boats, the lighting of the town's official tree and a town that had gone over-the-top with Christmas lights. A place where two of her new friends lived in a converted lighthouse. A town where a group of kooky senior citizens had made her an honorary member of their poetry club and bought her baby a crib.

The theme of the book stirred up emotions and many mothers in the room wiped at their eyes. Inevitably, Stacy's thoughts turned to her mother. She'd end the standoff tonight and make the first phone call. That much she'd come to accept. Stacy couldn't imagine being separated from her child for even a day at this point, but definitely not on Christmas.

Even if her mother hadn't provided an example to her of healthy love, she'd tried her best.

Stacy didn't doubt that her mother loved her the only way she knew how. She'd been the one to read to Stacy every night, encouraging a lifelong love affair with books. Nobody was perfect, and Stacy figured that she wouldn't be a perfect mother, either. For whatever mistakes she made, she hoped that her love would be enough to compensate. Because she already loved her little bean with all her heart.

After all of the books were read, the children were given candy canes, with Ava handing them out.

"Our best customer," Mr. Finch announced loudly when Stacy paid for the ten books from the wish tree.

The kids went home with their parents and the rest of the grown-ups headed to the Salty Dog for drinks. When they arrived at the bar, the mood was jovial and celebratory, and nearly every table was full. Debbie led them all to a table, but because they had such a large group, Stacy, Valerie and Ava let the seniors have the table and headed over to find empty stools at the bar.

"'Tis the season," Valerie said. "It's been slammed like this for days. Lots of office Christmas parties."

Cole and Max were behind the bar, serving up drinks, as, not surprisingly, many patrons were drinking. Two minutes later, Valerie went behind the bar to help. She served up coffee with Kahlúa for Ava, and a Coke for Stacy. Then she went down the line and helped those who didn't need a mixed drink or anything too fancy.

"How are you and Adam getting along?" Ava took a sip of her coffee.

"Great."

Stacy wasn't one to get too raunchy and most of what she had to share happened to be practically X-rated. Last night, they'd had sex under the Christmas tree just for kicks. This morning, Stacy found pine needles in her hair, and...other interesting places. Totally worth it.

"I know this wasn't planned or anything, but you two just seem made for each other." Ava smiled in Max's direction. "Just like me and Max. I love him bunches."

"It shows. Um, so do you know much about Adam's first wife?"

"Just that they were married a short time, and it was just heartbreaking the way she died." But Ava wouldn't meet Stacy's eyes.

There was more. Stacy had once studied human gestures—a crash course so that she could better write the antihero in her thrillers. And Ava had just indulged in a classic: eye-contact avoidance. If she'd been a person who normally did this, Stacy wouldn't think anything of it. But Ava was a bright and shiny light who always met Stacy's eyes.

"I haven't wanted to press Adam. I've a feeling it's still a pretty painful subject."

"Can I tell you something?" This time, Ava met

Stacy's eyes. Dead on. "I can only imagine what I'd feel like if Max had loved and lost someone before we met. But Mandy is someone Adam loved for an unfortunately short while, and you and he could have a lifetime of love ahead of you. You're making him a father for the first time."

"It's not that. We're still getting to know each other in many ways, but he's not one to talk about his feelings. I mean, maybe his former wife knew how to draw him out."

"Or maybe she didn't, either. I think Mandy was someone who had very good intentions, but she wound up putting Adam last. At least, that's what I've heard." She waved her hand dismissively. "I've already said too much. Ignore me."

"No, it's fine. Honestly, when I first decided to stay, it was mostly to help Adam. He sometimes gets this far-off look in his eyes like he's somewhere else. Like he's reliving a painful memory."

"I've seen that, too." Ava nodded. "But a whole lot less since you arrived."

It was good to hear.

"Well, I guess we're a distraction for him, that's true."

She'd made certain to keep his attention every time they made love. To hold his gaze when he thrust into her. She'd never sensed any hesitancy or dazed, faraway looks when he was with her, inside of her. That would have been a deal breaker.

"Hey, does anyone need the chef?" It was Adam's

warm voice as he wrapped his arms around Stacy's waist from behind.

"She definitely does!" Ava laughed and pointed.

Stacy turned to take in Adam. She'd never seen a man look that good in an apron, but Adam pulled it off and then some. He was wearing a T-shirt, his long, sinewy arms bunching under her touch.

"How was the reading? I'm sorry I missed it." His eyes were shimmering and warm.

"Stacy had those kids entranced when she read to them. I had no idea you were such a good speaker."

Stacy winked. "Special secret skill of mine."

"She has a lot of secret skills, actually." Adam grinned mischievously.

Stacy elbowed him in the gut. "Watch it, now."

"Oh, I am." He made a move as if to check out her backside. "Every chance I get."

"Y'all are making me so horny." Ava fanned herself. "Max, baby! Take me to bed right now!"

Max squinted as he filled a glass of wine, shook his head and pointed to his ear.

"Just my luck." Ava laughed.

"Ask him later. Pretty sure he won't shake his head again." Adam squeezed Stacy's hand. "I better get back to work."

Stacy watched as Adam walked away, the apron doing a fine job of framing a spectacular male behind. No fewer than five women watched him walk away.

"Perils of falling for a handsome man." Ava elbowed Stacy. "But I wouldn't trade it."

"Amen, sister."

And they both had a long laugh.

Later that night, Stacy waited up for Adam. In a few days, it would be Christmas Eve and a party with his friends at the lighthouse. The Salty Dog would be closed for Christmas. She looked forward to spending the entire day with Adam talking about their plans. Maybe doing some online shopping for the baby. Of course, she also had some writing to do, which she'd neglected lately, as she'd been otherwise occupied getting her fill of Adam.

Deciding it was time to get ready for bed, she brushed her teeth, brushed her hair and sat cross-legged in front of her first tree as a married woman. Adam had surprised her with this very tree, dragging it in behind him, a big smile on his face. A moment she'd never forget.

Memories rolled through of the first time she'd ever had a conversation with Adam. Of the first time she shocked him by letting him know that he'd be a father. Of their first dance together as a married couple, dancing to "Tennessee Whiskey." So much had happened to her in the last few months. First, she'd been knocked up, then gotten herself married and, last but not least, fallen in love. Exactly the reverse order of the conventional, but it worked for her.

She'd had an unconventional childhood, after all, and turned out just fine. Speaking of unconventional childhoods, Stacy picked up her cell and dialed her mother.

"Stacy? Is everything all right?"

"I'm fine, Mom. We're fine. I wanted to say hello."

"Oh, well." She sighed. "I was going to call you on Christmas Day."

"You were?"

"Of course. I don't want to be angry anymore."

Stacy waited a beat for the apology that should be coming, but when it didn't come, she came to a realization. She would do this one last time—reach out to the mother that wanted everything her way. Maybe if she did, *without* sliding back into old patterns, it might be the last time.

"I had a reading tonight and thought of you. Look, I know that you love me, I've always known. And I know how hard all this must be for you. The closer I get to being a mother, the more I think I understand. I'm sure you were always worried that I'd be hurt, or that someone would break my heart. But you did a good job raising me, both you and Nana."

"I miss those times. Gosh, I miss her so much. Every day."

Stacy pushed back tears with the pads of her fingers and choked back the emotion in her throat.

"So do I. She was really the glue that held us together, wasn't she?"

"*She* knew how to love."

Stacy took a deep breath. "Mom, I'm in love with Adam."

"Oh, *Stacy.*"

"I don't know what will happen, or where we will live, or even if he loves me back, but either way he's going to be in my life for what I hope will be a life-time."

"I do hope it works out for you. It isn't that I don't want that, because I do. But the thought of you hurting, the thought of you being so far away, where I can't even hug you…*that's* tough. At least after Daniel and Dominique," she said, spitting out their names, "I could be there for you. Hold you, comfort you, let you know you'd survive those two jack-asses."

"I know. And I put you through a lot over the years, oversharing."

She chuckled. "True enough. Sometimes ignorance is bliss. Any mother wants her child to be happy and safe, and it's impossible to forgive someone who has hurt your baby. Remember that. Your grandmother once said that she never told *her* mother when she had a fight with my father. She knew that she would forgive him easily, but the same couldn't be said of her mother."

"That makes all the sense in the world."

Stacy spoke to her mother for a few more minutes, all the worry and sadness slowly spooling out of her. It would be Christmas soon, and no better time to forgive. After she hung up, Stacy curled on the couch, calm and soothed. Peaceful. She honestly didn't think she could wait a few more days to give Adam her small present.

She fell asleep waiting for Adam, like a child waiting for Santa Claus.

Chapter Nineteen

Adam didn't get a chance to see Stacy again before the gang left. They'd been slammed at every turn. If he wasn't the head cook, and about to become an owner, he'd probably have had his ass handed to him for taking the short break he had. He made up for it when he got back, filling orders and working fast on his feet. The special barbecue rack of ribs that Adam had added to the menu for the holidays was the number-one request of the evening.

Later, after closing, Adam was on his way out the door when Cole stopped him.

"Hey. Can I talk to you in the office?"

"Yeah." Adam headed back, bending to pet Sub, who rolled over and showed his soft underbelly.

"Something came for you earlier today." Cole handed Adam an envelope.

He took it, an official-looking letter from the life-insurance company. Mandy's death benefit.

"Is that what I think it is?" Cole leaned back on the chair behind his desk.

As if his friend already knew the answer to the question, he dug in his drawer for a flask and set it on the desk.

Adam turned it over in his hands, the check that would be his reward for having been Mandy's husband for a short while.

"Yeah."

Cole poured from the flask into a shot glass and handed it to Adam. "You okay?"

Adam accepted the drink and drained it. "I'll be fine."

"You can talk about it, you know. If not to me, or Max, then…"

"To Stacy?"

But Cole and Max wouldn't understand. Adam couldn't afford to let his emotions get the better of him ever again. No more rage. The emotion had to be killed, restrained, because anger was a funny thing. Even when valid, it could hurt people just as surely as an air strike.

"Stacy needs me to be calm right now. She doesn't need any kind of emotional stress during the pregnancy."

"She needs you to *talk* to her. To let her in and be

honest. To tell her everything you're carrying around with you because she deserves to know all of who you are."

"So, I should tell her how I made my first wife feel useless? How I never put her first and took everything we had for granted? If she hadn't died, I'm not sure Mandy and I would have made it. We weren't in a good place. Stacy and I are newlyweds. I don't want her to leave me."

"Whether or not you realize it, you wear your guilt like a jacket. You never take it off, and it *shows*."

"What's that supposed to mean?"

"It means she must already know something is wrong."

"But I'm not the same since she got here."

"I know that, bro. She's the reason that check was even processed."

Cole was right. Stacy was the reason for everything, and didn't that scare the piss out of him? Was he really doing this again, letting someone into his heart? Was he going to risk losing her, even if through something as simple and common as a divorce?

No wonder his friends had been so worried about him. He'd rushed into marriage, leaped straight into a committed relationship with someone he barely knew. He wanted to believe Stacy was in this marriage with him and as bound to him as he was to her. But the reality was he'd talked her into this marriage. Just because things were good now didn't mean she would stay with him. It didn't mean he had her forever. He had to remember that.

Adam tore open the envelope and read the sum of money for his spousal benefit. It was certainly enough for Adam to buy in to the Salty Dog, with plenty left over for a security cushion.

"It's time for me to stop drifting. I'm having a child and I have a mission. I need a new plan. There's college, there's probably a bunch of other expensive crap that I don't even know about yet."

"I've wanted you to be a part of this venture of ours all along. But you're still riddled with guilt, and that bothers me."

"I don't know if I'll ever be able to let go of that completely, but I'm going to live my life, anyway. I have a lot to live for."

"I'm glad you finally accepted the insurance payout, but did you do this because you deserve it, or because someone you love needs the money?"

Adam folded the check and palmed it into his pocket. He didn't have an answer to Cole's question.

Driving home, Adam's thoughts turned to Stacy. She'd sweetly supported him all along, staying with him, never pushing him too hard. Only she had the ability to pull him away from bad memories with a single touch. Her voice always brought him back to where he *wanted* to be. To where he'd dreamed of staying. She'd rescued *him* the night they'd met, a hard pill to swallow for someone who lived to do the rescuing. She'd showed him that he hadn't forgotten how to feel. He was not so numb that Stacy couldn't reach him, because she had, and he'd never been the same.

He found Stacy asleep on the couch, the Christmas tree lights on and blinking in their synchronized pattern. Sitting beside her, he tugged her into his lap.

She woke almost immediately, rubbing her eyes in that way that reminded him of a newborn kitten. "Hi."

She buried her face in his neck, a habit that always wound up warming him more than it probably did her. "I can't wait for Christmas, to give you my gift. We weren't going to buy anything for each other this year, but…"

"Yeah, I didn't take that seriously, either."

She pulled back and chucked his shoulder. "Aw. But you know, mine is very small. Just very personal."

"Is it lingerie?"

She quirked an eyebrow. "That would be a gift for me."

"Let's be honest. It would be a gift for *me*."

"Okay, smart aleck." She crawled out of his lap and went for a small box under the tree.

"*Small* lingerie," he teased as he accepted the wrapped gift and shook it once. "Is it edible?"

"Try again." She watched him with nothing less than giddy anticipation in her eyes as he tore open the wrapping paper.

He removed the cover of the small white box to

find a beautiful tree ornament. Bright colors decorated a cottage-style home with Welcome painted on the red front door. Just like what one might see on the inside of a snow globe. And the writing below the ornament said Our First Christmas Together, and the year.

"It's more *specific*, for this year, so I thought… I thought you'd like it."

Adam didn't realize until she spoke that he'd been staring at it in a daze. For reasons he couldn't begin to understand, the ornament reminded him of failure. He'd failed at his first marriage, and not just because of those last ugly words. The fact remained that he'd put his career in the Navy ahead of everything and nothing had mattered more to him than the brotherhood. Nothing.

This wonderful woman—his wife—and their child were in his life, but for how long? How would he blow it this time? He had a second chance he didn't deserve, and he could easily ruin this, too, if he didn't snap out of it. Damn, the fear of loss gripped him like tentacles.

"Adam?"

He met Stacy's eyes, the hurt and pain radiating in them, thick and raw.

"It's really nice. I like it," he said, and tried to tug her close.

She wasn't having any of it, and he couldn't blame her. She shoved him away.

"This was supposed to be a reminder that *we're*

starting over fresh. *Our* first Christmas. You're still not here with me, are you?"

"I'm right here."

"Your body is, yes. I can have your body every night and you're with me then. But I need all of you, Adam. I need your heart and soul, and you're still not willing to open wide enough and let the past go."

"I am. You and the baby are all I want. You mean everything to me. I *have* to let the past go."

"No, you don't *have* to do anything besides be our baby's father. It turns out I was just fooling myself. But I've already been someone's second choice and I won't do it again."

It was as if she didn't hear him. "Stacy, don't be ridiculous. This is not about choices."

"No, of course not. There *is* no real choice for you. It's me and our baby, sort of a package deal. There was never any real choice, not for you."

"Why is it wrong for me to want you *both*? I'm happy about the baby. That doesn't mean I don't—" The word, which he meant with everything he had, sat on the edge of his tongue. Paralyzed.

The word is love. You love her, genius! Say it!

"Don't what?"

"It doesn't mean I don't want you, too. You have to know that."

Coward. Even he knew this fight was about more than this gift. She wanted him to say he loved her, to open up his heart and bleed for her. He wanted to, and in so many ways he already had.

"I don't know that at all." She crossed her arms. "You're too *nice* sometimes. Too perfect. Nobody's perfect, but I thought we had something here, something real."

"We do!"

She was everything he wanted. The future that he reached for every day. Right now, his future appeared to be a billow of smoke slowly evaporating. All because his heart and his mind were no longer in sync.

"Adam, my ex thought he loved me, too. He loved the life we had together, but he didn't love *me*. He loved his *ex-wife*, and even though they'd been apart for years when I met him, she was never fully out of his system. After investing so much in him, I wasn't enough."

"That's not me. Don't confuse me with that idiot."

"I fully take the blame here. It's like a sickness with me. I *saw* you were hurting, and I wanted to fix you. I wanted to fix you for our baby, so that you could be a better father. But I never planned on falling in love." She covered her face with both hands. "Oh, my God, I can't believe I did it again. Why do I keep *doing* this?"

He reached for her and she pushed him away. "You haven't done anything wrong. It's my fault."

"You *would* say that. Now it's probably also your fault that you can't love me. I know that you're still hurting. I can't imagine how hard it must be to love and lose someone." She turned in a circle as if she didn't know which way to go. "But I thought I'd pulled you out of the darkness. I can't do this anymore. I can't."

Adam's chest ached like someone had pierced it with an ice pick. "You can't do *what*?"

"I can't be responsible for your happiness. It's not my job to fix you. I'm not going to stay here with you and wait until you decide to love me." Her voice broke on the last few words and she may as well have ripped his heart out of his chest and stomped all over it with combat boots.

"You don't have to fix me. You don't have to *wait* for anything."

Desperation clouded his vision because he was losing her. And the irony of the whole damn thing was he was losing her because he was afraid of losing her. Talk about circular reasoning.

Fear clawing at him, he pulled her to him by her elbows. The sharp intensity of this moment had the words finally rushing out of him. "I love you, Stacy."

She gazed at him, her eyes filled with kindness and warmth. "I know you want to, honey. You want to more than anything, but you can't change what you don't acknowledge."

"That's not fair. How am I supposed to prove that I love you beyond everything that I've already done?"

She shook her head, tears rolling down her cheeks. "I don't know if you can."

"I've done everything anyone could ask for and more. I'm *here* for you."

She was quiet for several long and interminable

minutes as all the blood seemed to slowly leave his body. His heart was a slow thud in his chest that was beating only out of force of habit.

"Actually, you're not. Not all of you. I want your heart, Adam. I need you to bleed for me like I do for you. You're the love of my life, and I wanted to be yours."

She walked out of the room, shaking her head.

"Where are you going? We're not done here." He followed her and found her pulling a suitcase from under the bed. She began throwing clothes inside.

The tentacles spread over his heart, and surely his entire nervous system. He could barely move.

"I can't stay here."

He was furious both at himself and at her. Maybe he hadn't been completely honest with her about his feelings, but neither had she. She should have told him about that idiot ex of hers sooner. Had he known sooner that she'd felt second best once before, he could have proved to her she wasn't. She never could be.

Now he was working from a position of trying to make up for lost ground.

"It's almost Christmas! You're really going to leave me because I froze when I saw your gift?" He seemed to be yelling now.

"We both know that's not what we're fighting about." Her voice shook, but she spoke firmly, as if she wasn't tearing his heart out by its ventricles.

"Stacy, c'mon!"

God, she was *leaving* him. Leaving after all this. After he'd cracked open his heart like a walnut. He'd told her he loved her, and he did. But what good had it done him?

Was she going to spend the night in an airport? He couldn't let this happen. She walked right past him and continued out the front door, crossed the shared lawn to Susannah's house and knocked on her door.

"Seriously?" Adam stood outside watching it all unfold before his eyes.

Susannah opened her door, took one long look at the suitcase, and then another at him. She stepped aside and let in Stacy.

He wanted to grab Stacy like a caveman and drag her back into the house where she belonged. She was being ridiculous, possibly hormonal—hell, he didn't know!

But just before Christmas, he was alone again. Adam slammed the door shut.

Merry freaking Christmas.

"Thanks for letting me spend the night," Stacy said between sniffles. "I feel so guilty waking you up."

Susannah was wearing her fuzzy yellow bathrobe and matching slippers in the shape of ducks. She'd already gone to bed, and her hair was set in rollers. No wonder Susannah's hair was always so perfectly coiffed.

"What happened, honey? Did he buy you a vacuum cleaner for Christmas?"

"Nothing like that, no. Don't worry. I won't be here too long."

How Stacy wished it could have been something as simple as an unromantic or thoughtless gift. Instead, she'd had to watch as he slipped away from her all over again. She'd had to see him go to another place with yet another piercing memory. Maybe the ornament had been asking for too much, too soon. But no. She *deserved* a husband who loved her, who could open his heart big enough to let her inside. She refused to put herself through this agony anymore.

Susannah handed over a box of tissues. "I'm sure Adam will be over tomorrow morning, full of apologies. Sometimes it just takes a night apart to realize how much you love each other."

"Yeah. Sure." She dabbed at her eyes again.

Her chest physically ached, like someone had kicked her heart.

His name is Adam Cruz. Just the look on his face when he'd seen the ornament. She'd felt like an idiot, assuming this would be a highly sentimental gift. Instead, his reaction confirmed every one of her worst fears. He'd never be fully hers. And she had to stop trying before she wound up being last even with herself.

Susannah offered Stacy another plate of cookies, but she had no appetite. Still, she took one and made a half-hearted attempt. She adored and appreciated Susannah, a substitute grandmother when Stacy couldn't face calling her own mother. Just earlier tonight she'd told her mother that she'd fallen in love with Adam. It was too soon to tell her the truth, and maybe she never would. Adam was still her baby's father. He always would be.

She remembered Mom's words and Nana's sage advice. Apparently, no one else had followed the advice since then. No, she wouldn't complain to her mother about Adam. Even if she was truly done with him. Because there was still their baby.

Her cell had started to ping only a few minutes after she'd been inside. Adam, probably, but she refused to look. She wasn't hiding from him. He knew exactly where she was, and that she was safe, although he was probably wondering if she had a plan. She had none. She was going to stay here until she could figure it out, hopefully sometime tomorrow.

"Do you want to talk about it?" Susannah's voice was so warm and soothing that Stacy felt compelled to talk.

"I don't know if it will help."

Doodle jumped up in the woman's arms and she rubbed between his ears. "Doodle is going to be an emotional-therapy dog, I've decided. You just can't feel sad with Doodle in your lap."

"Doodle in your lap?" Stacy actually cracked a smile. "That's wordplay, whether you realize it or not."

"Why do you think I named him Doodle?" She

stood, held out the small poodle and plopped him in Stacy's lap. "Give him a little rub. You'll feel better."

Stacy didn't know how to break this to her neighbor, but a cute doggy would not solve her problems. Still, she tried, with slow pats between his ears. "Hi, Doodle."

The dog looked from Stacy to Susannah and back to Stacy. Apparently realizing he had no choice, because the sad pregnant lady needed him, he settled down in her lap to snooze. So, she was even second best with a dog.

"What stupid thing did Adam do?" Susannah asked.

"It wasn't stupid. Adam is perfect. He just can't help this one thing but it's not his fault. Not entirely."

"And what's the one thing that isn't his fault?"

"He *had* to marry me because I'm pregnant."

And then Stacy explained it all. The first time she'd seen Adam zone out with the first-Christmas ornament on the night of the tree lighting. How she'd believed and hoped she'd finally drawn him out of that dark place, and then, tonight's disaster. The ornament. His dull, lost, pained expression. Stacy's belief that he was still hurting for his late wife and couldn't move on.

"Are you sure that's why he zoned out?" Susannah cocked her head. "Could it be something else?"

"Like what? It's not like he would *tell* me. I've tried to draw him out, to get him to talk to me. But Adam doesn't talk about his feelings."

"If he even *understands* his feelings." Susannah

nibbled on a cookie. "Of course, there's always the possibility this has nothing to do with you. Not everything is about you."

Susannah probably hadn't meant to be rude, but the words felt like a slap. "I know. It's about someone else who is *not* me. Mandy, his first wife."

"Or maybe this is about *Adam*. His thing. His pain. And it has nothing to do with either one of you."

She'd considered Adam could be suffering from some residual PTSD from his service. It was possible she'd assumed he was thinking of his first wife, but on the other hand, the first-Christmas ornament was a dead giveaway. She'd been an idiot to give him an ornament, all bright and sparkling new, like that could change everything.

"He said he loved me."

Susannah brightened. "Well, that's something!"

"It would have meant more had he not said it while trying to end an argument."

"He said it, dear, and Adam doesn't strike me as the kind of man who says those words casually."

"He wants to love me, I know. I'm the mother of his child and Adam always does the right thing. Always. His loyalty and honor are above reproach."

"But...?"

"I want his heart. His whole heart. And I deserve nothing less. I'm Stacy Harts—um, Cruz, aka Piper Lawrence, damn it, and I want all of him." She sat up straight and tall.

She was proud of her work, and that she'd succeeded in an area where most never did. Every day she bled words all over the screen. She might make her money writing thrillers, but she would not write for anything less than love for the written word.

"Yes, you do." Susannah patted Stacy's knee. "And you'll have him."

"Do you know that he never even asked me to marry him? It was an offer. A suggestion. This marriage was one of convenience and that was okay then. It's just that things have changed. For me." Stacy yawned and rubbed one eye. "Do you mind if I go to bed? It's a little late for me."

Susannah grabbed fresh sheets from the hallway linen closet and handed them to Stacy. "Things will be better in the morning. You'll see."

The spare bedroom Stacy entered was an explosion of Precious Moments figurines, just like Nana used to collect. They covered every spare inch of space. Bookshelves, dresser, nightstand.

"There are more in my bedroom. It was an obsession for a while," Susannah said, following Stacy's gaze.

"Reminds me of my Nana. I feel right at home," Stacy said good-night and closed the door.

Chapter Twenty

The next morning, Stacy woke to the sound of Susannah puttering in the kitchen, humming "Winter Wonderland."

She reached into her suitcase, where she'd packed her ratty robe and slippers, and a minute later padded down the hallway.

"Good morning."

"Did you sleep okay?" Hands busy with a spatula, Susannah nudged her chin toward a covered bowl on the breakfast nook. "Adam brought you breakfast. He was here only a few minutes ago. Told me to let you sleep."

There was a folded note taped to the tinfoil, her name scrawled in his handwriting. She opened it and read:

Stop being ridiculous. Answer my texts.

"He *says* I'm ridiculous." Stacy ripped the note in two. Then she tore it into smaller pieces, shredded it, actually, and threw it in the trash can. "I'm not being ridiculous!"

"Oh, dear. What an unfortunate choice of words." Susannah shook her head.

"Words matter, don't they?"

"Yes, they do."

"I knew you would understand."

She uncovered the dish to find the oatmeal he made her each morning with milk, butter, brown sugar, cranberries, raisins and nuts. He already knew she was a creature of habit and had eaten this breakfast every morning since he first made it for her. Her favorite.

Stacy ignored the sweet ache that reminded her she loved him, damn it. The dummy. The idiot. The dummy idiot.

"So what are you going to do about this man who delivers breakfast, obviously adores you, is the father of your child, but calls you ridiculous?"

"I don't know yet, but I'll figure it out. Just give me the day. That's my self-imposed deadline."

"Oh, sugar, take all the time you need. I love the company. So does Doodle." She bent and offered him a piece of bacon. "Don't you, Doodle?"

Doodle practically snapped Susannah's fingers off as he took the bacon and trotted away.

"I have some writing to do. Don't let me get in your way."

She'd been neglecting her daily word count and her new book was practically on life support. Thanks to Adam, and all his alluring ways to draw her away from writing.

Even if all he'd had to do was enter the room.

After eating her breakfast, Stacy retreated to the spare bedroom and wrote like the wind, the words slicing through her like they were just being poured down from heaven. Sometimes, it was this easy. She'd plotted this book in advance, and she knew everything that would happen before it did. If only life could be as simple as a book she'd plotted in advance.

Had she been able to plot her romance with Adam, she'd have had a "meet cute" in that hole-in-the-wall bar in Marion. She would step out of her comfort zone and introduce herself. Talk to the lonely-looking guy who was far too handsome for his own good. They would date for a few months and by the time they slept together around the midway point of the story, the wedding photo would have been put away in a keepsake box.

They would have fallen in love, on or close to the same time. Then when she'd become pregnant in an unexpected twist, love and marriage would have naturally followed. Maybe.

But, try as she might, Stacy couldn't write a love story to save her life.

* * *

Adam slammed around the kitchen of the Salty Dog all morning. Brian eyed him with suspicion, as if maybe he'd been body-snatched with someone who simply looked like Adam. And he understood why. He'd kept his anger under tight control for months. No, try years.

Today, he was about one nanosecond away from losing his collective shit.

And as if the universe knew Adam Cruz was on his last nerve, the entire town of Charming decided they wanted lunch at the Salty Dog. All at the same time.

"How's that order coming, Adam?" Valerie called out.

"It's coming," he muttered, chopping away.

"We've got a line out the door, and Max wants us getting them fed and out so more can come in."

"Of course, he does."

Everyone was so damn freaking cheerful. Eating, drinking, making merry and opening presents.

He couldn't stand it.

"What's eating you?" Brian started the timer on the fryer again. "All this traffic is good for business."

"Yeah, I'm happy. Why? Don't I *look* happy?" Adam brandished the knife he'd just used to separate a rack of ribs.

"Um, yeah, boss. You look ecstatic. How about me?" He grinned, put his thumbs up and then did a moon walk across the floor, making Adam almost smile. Almost.

He could see now, hindsight being twenty-twenty, that maybe he shouldn't have told Stacy he loved her to end a fight. But he *did* love her, damn it, more than he ever dreamed possible. A love so easy and comfortable that he hadn't even realized when he'd fallen in love. This time around love was different. She felt like his soul mate, if there was such a thing. He loved her strength and independence. He appreciated her resilience and the way she didn't need him, but accepted him into her life, anyway. She'd made room for him and she didn't have to.

His love for her was a mature and selfless one, stronger than he'd ever believed possible.

The guilt that spiked through him now was a different kind. It was no longer from a man who had said ugly last words to the wife he'd taken for granted.

Now he was guilty of moving on, of loving someone else, of getting a second chance at a full life. In Mandy, he had somehow memorialized every young and healthy sailor or soldier that never got to come home. Young lives, snuffed out. The pervasive sadness of those losses threatened to cloud over and derail every grace ever handed to him. He wasn't at all sure *he* should have been the one allowed to return. But on the night he'd met Stacy, he'd been gifted with a second chance even if he hadn't realized it.

Frankly, he also believed there was such a thing

as justified anger. He had a right to his. Stacy had walked away from him because of one stupid moment. She should have stayed, and they could have talked it out. He deserved better than her leaving based on a stupid argument. He deserved better than her ignoring his messages.

During a temporary lull in the kitchen, Adam made a decision.

"I need a break." He ripped off his apron. "And I'm taking it now."

"Great. I've asked you five times whether you were ever going to take a break," Brian said.

Adam pulled out his cell, but he still did not have a response to the dozens of text messages he'd left Stacy. Unacceptable.

She wanted him to talk about his feelings. Well, he was going to give her some of his *feelings* all right. He drove home, his anger simmering somewhere between nuclear threat and the heat of a thousand suns.

When he arrived, he stalked over to Susannah's house and pounded on her front door. Her little dog began to bark in alarm.

Susannah opened the door. "Oh, hello, Adam."

"I'm here to talk to Stacy and I'm not leaving until I do."

"Stacy?" Susannah called out as she turned around. "Adam is here."

"I don't want to talk. Go away, Adam."

"Tell her I'm not going anywhere." He crossed his arms. "I'll stay here all day if I have to."

"Stacy, now, please be reasonable. There's absolutely no harm in talking." Susannah picked up her poodle, who looked ready to seize. "This is quite upsetting to Doodle."

"Tell Adam I can't even look at him right now," Stacy said.

"Tell her she doesn't have to look at me," Adam said. "And also, this is ridiculous."

This went on back and forth between them until Susannah held up her index finger in a motion for Adam to wait. She then shut the door. About two minutes later, it opened again, and Stacy was gently pushed out.

Her arms were crossed. "You're disturbing Doodle. He has anxieties."

"This will be quick," Adam said, struggling to tamp down his anger enough to speak actual words instead of grunts. "You said you wanted my heart, and other than having it surgically removed and placing it right in your hands, I don't know what more I can do to show that you already have it. But you also said you wanted me to talk about my feelings. I can do that."

"Really?" She quirked an eyebrow.

"But you're not going to like this. See, I wasn't a very good husband the first time around. Probably didn't talk about my feelings then, either. If you want to know the truth, I'm not even sure Mandy and I would have made it through another year together had she lived. She wasn't too thrilled with me most of the time. And then there was our last conversation—"

Stacy's entire posture changed, and she straightened, holding up her palm. "You don't have to—"

"The hell I don't. You wanted this—well, you got it. The last words I said to Mandy were ugly and hurtful ones. I was angry because she and the other doctors were going straight into enemy territory. And I was the big bad SEAL who told her we didn't want or need their help. To tell the truth, I didn't have a heart to help anyone. I wanted to kill the enemy and protect my brothers. And it's that simple. No room for anyone else. Not the news cameras, not the doctors and nurses. I didn't know she was going to die, but she did, and those were the last words I ever said to her."

"Adam... I'm so sorry."

"That's *why* I kept her picture, to remind me that I'd failed and didn't deserve to try again. I know how much words can hurt. Sometimes, you don't get a chance to take them back. You want to know my feelings? I'm pretty damn mad at you. You were the one who walked away from me when you *should* have stayed."

"I—I..." For once, she seemed speechless.

Because he was right, and on a roll.

"Is that what you're going to do every time we have a big fight? Leave me? Because that's a pretty lousy commitment. I may not be the world's most touchy-feely guy but if there's one thing I understand well its loyalty and commitment. I'm your husband, damn it, and you failed me. You left without giving me much of a chance to fix anything."

"I'm sorry. I didn't think. I…"

"That's not much of an excuse."

She tipped her chin. "Maybe not, but you *should* have told me all of this and not left me scrambling in the dark, trying to uncover the mystery that is Adam Cruz!"

"And I would have if you'd given me a little more time. We just got married, so forgive me if I didn't want to hand you a list of my many failures." He turned. "Now I'm going inside, where I'm going to take apart the Christmas tree and string the lights the way I want them."

And with that, he stomped away.

Stacy had never seen Adam this angry, but with a sudden rush of regret she acknowledged he had every right. Now he'd told her where his pain and memories came from. They were based around *guilt*, not love. He'd been hanging on to the regret he felt for having *hurt* Mandy before she died. No wonder she'd rarely seen a hint of anger in him.

He was scared he'd say something to hurt Stacy, too.

"What did he say?" Susannah asked when Stacy stepped inside.

"He's angry."

"I saw that. But surely you apologized for walking out on him, right?"

Dear God, even Susannah. "I didn't. But… I will."

You do this every time, Stacy. When things go wrong, you walk away. But it won't be easy to walk away from a marriage.

Her mother's words reverberated. Stacy had always walked away from relationships when a conflict came up. With Daniel, even though she would have been an idiot to stay with him, she'd never even heard him out. Never gave him a chance to truly apologize, never heard why he'd given up on them. She'd simply walked away and never looked back. She hadn't ever needed a man and prided herself on the fact. She was always the first to walk away. There were usually good reasons, or at least they seemed so at the time. But other than to her family, and her work, she'd never learned true commitment.

Even with her mother, she'd been passive-aggressive, moving to another state rather than setting boundaries.

Now, she'd fallen in love deeply and completely, and possessed zero conflict-resolution skills.

She'd been so caught up in her hang-ups about being second best again, she'd neglected to examine herself. Yes, she'd been right about asking him to open up, because if he had it might have made all the difference. But she'd been wrong about being his second choice. Even though he'd try telling her, she hadn't listened. Susannah was right. The dazed look she'd witnessed, this was all Adam's pain, and had nothing to do with Stacy or anyone else.

"I don't know how to fix this," Stacy said. "I ruined us."

"Oh, don't be so dramatic. If he's mad, he'll calm down. Then you go and talk to him."

"If he'll listen."

"Well, honey, he found a way to get you to listen to him. I think you can do the same." Susannah patted the empty space next to her on the couch. "You've both had a crash course in love, babies and family. It's no wonder you've had a few growing pains."

"This really is our first fight." Pregnant, married for just over a week and they'd just had their first real fight. "Should I go over there right now?"

"Give it a day. And when you talk again, make it good. Make sure he knows how much you love him."

"If I haven't already lost him."

Chapter Twenty-One

On Christmas Eve morning, Stacy woke with her baby pressing so hard on her bladder it felt like she might be auditioning for the Olympic gymnastics team. She ran to the bathroom, then curled back into bed, covering her head with the blanket because she was not ready to face the day. But it was Christmas Eve, and next door, she still had presents to wrap. She and Adam had plans to be at the lighthouse this evening for a gift exchange with his friends. Now she had no idea what would happen.

She picked up her cell to find no more texts from Adam. He'd given up on her. She finally answered the last one, where he'd asked her again to please come home. She texted:

Okay.

After fifteen minutes, she still had no reply. Not even three little dots showing a text was coming. Adam never slept past 6:00 a.m., so Stacy eventually heaved out of bed again and peeked out the front window. His truck was gone from their driveway. Great. She could go home, of course, and be there when he got back. Pretend nothing happened and go back to her passive-aggressive way of dealing with conflict. Apologize, then slip right back into old patterns having resolved nothing. Easy-peasy.

Not this time.

She had to face this, dead-on.

I may not be the world's most touchy-feely guy, but I understand loyalty and commitment.

Adam's words. Last night, she'd come to a decision. She was fully committed to their marriage. Walking out in the middle of an argument had not been the way to show him.

Stacy started the coffee and made breakfast, realizing she literally hadn't cooked since her arrival in Charming. The thought brought out more emotional tears. Damn these hormones.

"Good morning," Susannah said. "My goodness, you didn't have to cook for me."

"I *have* to and you can't stop me." Stacy brandished the spatula. "I've been spoiled within an inch of my life. Do you know Adam hasn't let me to cook anything since I arrived?"

"What a horrible man." Susannah smirked. "Let's turn him into the authorities."

Stacy pulled out her tissue and wiped away more tears. "Oh, these darn hormones. I have never cried so much in my life. This isn't like me."

"Go ahead, sugar. Crying is good for the soul. Clears out all the cobwebs. I myself indulge at least once a month."

"Adam won't respond to my text message."

"*Message?* One?" Susannah poured herself a cup of coffee. "Give him time. Take your mind off your trouble. We're having a meeting of the Almost Dead Poet Society today and you can join us."

"I'm sorry to miss it."

"Oh, well, you can't very well miss it. It's going to be here."

"Here?"

"You could always go next door if you must, but this would be your first meeting as our in-house writer. We also have our gift exchange."

Stacy dropped the spatula. "But I don't have anything for y'all!"

"That's all right, dear. I tend to have plenty of backup gifts on hand. You can never be too prepared. I know you can find a little something for everyone in my stash."

Stacy hoped they weren't all Precious Moments figurines. Susannah dragged out her box. Inside it were dozens of specialty candles, ornaments, globes and boxes of candy. Peppermint, chocolate, caramels.

"I start shopping in August, then hit the after-Christmas sales and stock up."

Stacy picked a beautiful snow globe. A little town with a shining lighthouse.

"Oh, how did that get mixed up in here? This was going to be your gift," Susannah said.

Stacy shook it, then held it up, admiring. This was perfect.

"Is it okay with you if I give Adam my gift?"

"Of course, sugar. Just pick anything else in here you like. And I'll help wrap."

The senior citizens began to arrive around two, and Stacy prepared to be social for a few hours. Patsy bustled in with her walker. Lois and Mr. Finch arrived holding hands—so sweet—with Etta Mae right behind them.

"I've never been an in-house writer, so I don't know what you expect from me." Stacy helped Susannah bring the sweet tea and cookies into the living room, where they were all seated.

"Just sit, listen and enjoy, honey. You're more of an honorary member."

"But first, I have an announcement to make."

No more hiding to avoid conflict, or judgment. It was time to be up front with these good people.

"Go ahead." Susannah waved a hand.

Stacy splayed her palms wide. "We're all friends here, and you know me. I've been hiding something from some of you, and I don't want to do that anymore. The truth is that I write fiction under a pen name."

"An *alias*?" Etta Mae gasped.

"A *pen* name. I'm not hiding from the law. I write thrillers under the name Piper Lawrence and I'm proud to do it. I don't know how much they contribute to the literary world, but they're my personal not-so-guilty pleasure. And that of a few thousand readers. So that's why Susannah invited me to be your in-house writer."

"I *knew* you looked familiar!" Patsy snapped her fingers.

"Roy has that book." Lois nodded.

"Where can I find your book?" Etta Mae said. "Please don't tell me I have to order online."

"We might have a copy or two left at Once Upon a Book," Mr. Finch said.

The chatter went on for several minutes before Etta Mae managed to redirect them.

The afternoon began with Etta Mae's poem, "Ode to Christmas Shopping." Very timely. Mrs. Villanueva had a lovely poem about snuggling and hot sex in front of a roaring fire, and Susannah recited her latest poem about Doodle. This time it involved Doodle's relentless pursuit of a butterfly. The Doodle himself sat at attention under the table, salivating, hoping for a morsel of food to drop within his reach.

"We wrote this poem together." Lois elbowed Mr. Finch. "Right, sugar?"

Mr. Finch nodded as they both stood. "I call this one, 'Act Two.'"

The two recited the poem, each taking a turn with a verse. The stanzas were about love at the second stage of life. Having two great loves in a lifetime if you were lucky. About how one love never dulls another and how losing someone only makes you all the more appreciative the second time you fall in love. They stole loving looks at each other and everyone in the room realized who had fallen in love for the second time. This was their act two.

The applause for Lois and Mr. Finch filled the room, and they shared a chaste kiss.

The gift exchange began, and no one was surprised when Lois received a beautiful gold bracelet from Mr. Finch. The other gifts were more modest. Stacy bit back emotional tears when Mr. Finch gave her a coffee mug that read:

Please do not annoy the author. She might put you in a book and kill you.

She accepted a book of love poems from Mrs. Villanueva, a beautiful engraved fountain pen from Lois, a journal from Etta Mae and a T-shirt from Susannah with the words *Future New York Times best-selling author*. Stacy gave out the gifts she'd chosen and wrapped from Susannah's stash: ornaments, a candle and candy for Mr. Finch.

After everyone left, Stacy helped Susannah clean

up. Stacy checked, and there remained technological silence to her last text message to Adam. His truck was still gone, so Stacy had to decide whether she'd attend the gift exchange at Valerie and Cole's alone. In the end, the choice was simple. Whether Adam attended or not, she wanted to see Valerie, Cole and the rest of the gang.

This meant going next door to get her gifts and wrap them. The house was silent when she walked inside, with no sign of Adam. Naturally the kitchen was spotless, and their bed made. As promised, or threatened, he'd removed the tree lights and put everything back on in a haphazard way that almost drew a laugh out of her. Funny how two people could be so different about a tree and yet almost finish each other's sentences.

After changing into the only dress still fitting, Stacy grabbed the presents from the closet where she'd stored them, quickly wrapped them and piled them into her sedan. Either Adam would be there, or he wouldn't. He'd either be happy to see her, or ready for round two. The thought made her shake a little because Adam was correct. Anger was a powerful emotion, and she'd avoided highly intense confrontations for that reason. She didn't want to disrupt anyone else's peaceful holiday, but she wouldn't avoid Adam or anyone else.

That was the easy way.

When she arrived, Valerie opened the front door,

dressed to kill in a red dress with a tight bodice and black heels. Stacy felt positively matronly next to her.

"Hi! I was beginning to worry about you." She ushered Stacy in, helping with the gifts. "Adam is already here."

"I—I had to attend the poetry meeting."

"That's what I figured. My grandma told me you'd be there."

The lighthouse had been transformed into a little winter wonderland. There were white fairy lights and green garland strung throughout, and a huge decorated tree to the side of the spiral staircase. "Let It Snow" drifted through the surround-sound speakers.

The last time she'd been here, she'd danced to "Tennessee Whiskey" in the center of the room with her new husband. Looking back, she'd already fallen in love with him, this loyal and dutiful man who would do right by her and their baby. Her feelings went far deeper than loyalty and duty, and at the time she hadn't dared to hope he felt the same way.

She spied Adam on the other side of the room talking animatedly with Max. Stacy thought it best to stay on her side of the room until she at least made eye contact with him. If they noticed anything wrong, Valerie and Ava didn't say. But, c'mon, how could they *not* notice? Adam had always been right beside her, doing his best to find ways to touch her even if it was just his hand lingering on her back.

Ava led Stacy to the buffet table set up with dips and chips, crackers, shrimp and other finger food.

Stacy didn't have much of an appetite, a rarity these days, but she made a half-hearted attempt at a tortilla chip. She kept the conversation light with Ava, discussing her elaborate wedding plans.

"I wanted to get married at City Hall, too, but my parents won't have it," she said. "I'm their only daughter, so—"

"Time for the gift exchange!" Valerie announced from the bottom of the staircase. "Santa will help."

Beside her, Cole wore a Santa hat and carried the big red bag. "Though we did a name exchange, Valerie and I have presents for all of you."

"Now before you say you didn't get me anything, it's been the most wonderful year of my life," Valerie said, "And I want to celebrate finding Cole again after so many years apart."

"High-school sweethearts, together again," Max shouted.

Cole handed out the wrapped gifts, starting with Adam, who was next to him. "I picked your name, so you have two. Oh, wait. Three."

He handed the wrapped snow globe from Stacy with the others. Her eyes were riveted to him as he opened that one first, shook it, then turned it over and read the note she'd written. He did meet her eyes then, those deep soulful eyes that would always haunt her.

She didn't break eye contact but let him see all the hurt and pain she felt at the thought of losing him. If she'd expected him to rush over to her and take her into his arms, that didn't happen. Instead, he fiddled inside his pocket and was interrupted by Brian.

Okay, so maybe this gift didn't mean anything to him, either. She'd failed to reach him yet again.

A little fresh air was needed. Turning, she ran out the front door before anyone could stop her.

I'm not leaving. I'm just walking outside, where I can breathe.

The evening stars were twinkling brightly, the gentle waves crashing.

"Stacy."

She turned and there stood Adam, hands shoved in the pockets of his jeans. The flashing outside lights splashed a kaleidoscope of colors over him. White, red, green, blue. Back to white again. And for only a brief moment, he resembled a dark and beautiful angel. Her whole heart buzzed with love.

His gaze met hers, and it felt like a cord pulled her to him.

"Did you mean it?"

The note she'd written and taped to the bottom of the globe had read:

I am fully committed to you.

"You took a chance on me. I'd never been married before, and I always had a bad habit of walking away every time things got too emotional but that stops now. It was hard for me to come here tonight, you know." Her breath hitched as her voice broke.

"I do know." He took a step toward her. "I've

made mistakes with you and I own them. Listen, for a long time, I felt guilty about coming home when too many others didn't. But for the last few weeks I've felt particularly guilty because I fell in love. I thought I knew what love was until I met you. You *are* the love of my life, Stacy. Believe it."

She rushed him then, just falling into his arms. "I love you, I love you, I love you."

"Okay, then please let me do this. I had a plan." He set her back a short distance, then went down on bended knee. "Stacy, would you marry me?"

"We're already married, honey."

"Yes, but I never asked you. I never officially proposed like a man in love should do."

"Adam, I'd marry you all over again."

"Great, because I also have your Christmas gift." He drew out a tiny box and presented her with a diamond ring. "It took me all day to find this. I drove for hours. I gave you a gold band on our wedding day, which seemed good enough at the time. Not good enough now. You need a diamond."

She held out her ring finger and let him slip it on. It was a beautiful shiny bauble and shimmered outside with the rest of the holiday lights. Like Adam, it was hers, and she would never give it up.

"I love you." He pressed her forehead to his. "You're my new beginning."

The words wrapped around her heart. Then he kissed her, and, in that kiss, he gifted her with the promise of a whole future.

Theirs.

Epilogue

Five months later

"Stacy? Baby, where's your bag?"

From the moment Stacy announced her water had broken, Adam frantically searched their bedroom, the garage, the baby's room and the kitchen. The place where Stacy had stashed her hospital overnight bag was a mystery. She'd been in charge of the bag and the baby.

He had everything else.

"I've got it."

He turned and she stood behind him, clutching her small suitcase. She looked a sight, huge with his child, her hair sticking up on one side. She wore white Chucks and what she claimed was the only dress that still fit around her large belly and resembled a tent.

And she still took his breath.

"Give me that," he muttered, grabbed the bag from her and steered her to the front door.

Stacy groaned and Adam stopped moving. He'd been through dozens of missions and witnessed grown men weep, but he could not handle *Stacy* in any kind of pain. Unfortunately, he'd only discovered this thirty minutes ago, when her water broke. For the last few months, he'd been strategic about his mission to get her to Houston. He'd charted different routes at various times of the day, accounting for traffic, rainstorms, even a damn hurricane.

He had a *plan*. He was ready for anything, or so he thought.

And then Stacy's face scrunched up in pain and he felt useless. Helpless.

She clutched his arm, fingernails digging into his flesh, and groaned again. "Adam."

It was only then that he realized he'd been frozen next to her like a statue. Like a petrified and fossilized statue of a man who had zero clue.

He snapped out of it. "Okay, let's go. You ready for this?"

"No," she whined, and clutched his arm as he led her out the front door. "Honey, I'm scared."

"Don't worry, we practiced for this. We did the dry run."

"This feels really different." She huffed and waddled to the passenger-side door. "Did you call my mother?"

"Yeah, she said she'll meet us there."

"Oh, Stacy?" Susannah called out from next door. "Is this what I think it is? Finally time for the baby, or another practice run?"

"Is that another crack about me being late?" Stacy shook her fist. "The baby comes on her own timetable, Susannah!"

Stacy had been hypersensitive about going almost two weeks past her due date, as if she'd neglected to return a library book on time and couldn't stand the shaming.

"This is it." Adam shoved the suitcase in the back. "She's in labor. Water broke."

Susannah shut her front door and ran across the lawn to their driveway.

"What's happening?" Adam asked, as Susannah opened the rear-passenger door.

"I'm coming, of course. We all are. The entire Almost Dead Poet Society. We can't let you two do this alone."

"But *this* wasn't part of our dry run."

"Aren't you men so cute?" Susannah chuckled. "You think this is all going to go according to plan."

The entire drive to Houston, Susannah used her cell to alert all the seniors. Adam was shocked to learn that they'd had their own plans for months and were now putting them into motion. They planned to hold a sit-in, reciting poetry as his baby was born. Selections had been made months ago and included some of their own poems scattered with "the greats."

"You realize this could take a while." Adam pulled into the hospital parking lot several minutes later. "We could be here for hours. This is a first-time baby, and the doctor said it could be twenty-four hours for all we know."

Stacy made a caterwauling sound that almost rattled the windows. "Oh, God. I have to push."

"What?" All the blood drained from his body. "No, you *can't*. Not yet."

"Oh, dear," Susannah said. "This happened to my sister's daughter. Some women are superfast and efficient at labor. Way to go, Stacy!"

"No! Stop it. This is unacceptable."

"I'm sorry, honey." Stacy slid down the seat. "I'm trying."

Then there was nothing left for Adam to do but pick up his wife and jog to the emergency room.

Good thing Stacy had been wrong about having to push. With plenty of time to get up to the maternity ward, Tennessee Rose Cruz was born eight hours later. She weighed in at an impressive nine pounds, three ounces. Stacy's baby girl looked a lot like her father—her dark hair and eyes a perfect match.

Adam sat on a chair near Stacy's hospital bed and held their child, all swaddled in a blanket like a bean burrito. Only the top of her head showed, a little curl of dark hair.

Adam reached for Stacy's hand and squeezed it. "You did great."

"Liar."

She could smile now because the suffering was over. When those sudden first labor pains had wrapped around her back to her stomach, she didn't know who was more terrified, her, or Adam. Suddenly her big bad Navy SEAL was thrown for a loop. Turned out he couldn't stand to see his wife in physical pain. Rather sweet of him.

"The nurse said your labor progressed quickly for a first-timer." He took a moment to fist-bump Stacy with his free hand.

"Right on. I'm a star."

Instead of feeling tired, a surge of energy spiked through her, and she wondered if she'd be able to sleep at all.

"We have a crowd that's been patiently waiting for visiting hours."

"Have they really been here all day?"

"When I went out to report progress, Etta Mae was reciting 'Ode to New Life.' Your mother tried to beat a path into the delivery room, but I managed to talk her down."

"They can come in a few at a time," the nurse said. "As long as Mom is up to it."

"I'm fine. Go get my mother first."

Stacy accepted their little bundle from Adam.

She unwrapped the blanket enough to hold Tennessee's little hand, which opened and curled around Stacy's finger. A sweet rush of love and tenderness thrummed through her.

"Hello, my love. I'm never going to tell you how your daddy and I actually met. Okay?"

The curtain surrounding her bed swirled open and there stood her mother and Susannah with bright beaming faces.

"Can I hold her?" Mom asked, teary-eyed.

"Of course. Meet your granddaughter."

Mom expertly took the baby from Stacy and held her close, no doubt marveling at her incomparable beauty. Sure, maybe Stacy was a bit biased, but she believed that Tennessee was the most beautiful baby she'd ever seen. She'd heard some babies came out red and wrinkled but her baby girl was pink and perfect.

"And are we still sure about the name?" Mom looked up.

"Yes," Stacy and Adam said at once.

"You'll be happy to know our sit-in was a great success," Susannah said, admiring the tiny bundle. "We plan on doing it again sometime."

Adam quirked an eyebrow. "When?"

"Another baby is sure to come along," Susannah said. "Besides, we're responsible for three young people falling in love, thanks in large part to our poetry. But this is the first baby we can claim."

Stacy and Adam exchanged a quick glance and a

smirk. The society certainly hadn't done anything to assist with Tennessee's conception, or even with her parents falling in love. But there was no harm in it.

I love you, Adam silently mouthed.

Theirs was the beginning of a lifetime full of love.

* * * * *